## How to Catch a Prince
### (Even if your glass slipper is a size nine.)

**1)** Turn a tedious housekeeping job into an adventure by sneaking naps in the handsome owner's bed. (Getting caught by handsome owner would be even better!)

**2)** Turn a disaster like falling bottom-first into a cactus patch to your advantage. Have princely bachelor remove each needle with his own bare hands.

**3)** Turn bachelor's head away from thoughts of other women by cooking your way into his heart! (And conveniently "helping" other bride candidates cook their way *out* of the kitchen.)

**4)** Turn yourself into the fairy princess of his dreams by just being the wonderful gal that you are! (If he's a real prince, *he* won't be fooled by imitations.)

*Dear Reader,*

"Just friends." When you're talking men and women, those two words can mean exactly what they say, or they can hide a wealth of attraction underneath their bland exterior. I happen to be friends—*just* friends—with a couple of guys. They're great. They give me a whole different perspective on things like movies, and I can even go to them for interpretations of the male psyche when I have a date with a guy who seems to have come from an entirely different planet. But speaking of entirely different…that's the way to interpret "just friends" when you're talking about the hero and heroine of Shawna Delacorte's *Much Ado About Marriage*. They start out planning to keep things platonic, but…well, let's just say they don't succeed, and that what *does* happen is a whole lot more fun.

There's also fun in store in Linda Lewis's *Cinderella and the Texas Prince*. Seems there's a bit of competition going on at Travis Rule's ranch. The bride candidates are in residence—and in trouble. Because the unlikeliest woman of all seems to have the lead when it comes to winning the heart of the richest bachelor in Texas. Miss Cindy Ellerbee—the *housekeeper,* for heaven's sake!—is cooking and cleaning and *kissing* those other women right out of Travis's mind. Seems as if there's a Western wedding on the way.

Have fun with both these great books, and don't forget to come back next month for two more wonderful novels all about meeting—and marrying—Mr. Right.

Enjoy!

*Leslie Wainger*

Leslie Wainger
Senior Editor and Editorial Coordinator

Please address questions and book requests to:
Silhouette Reader Service
U.S.: 3010 Walden Ave., P.O. Box 1325, Buffalo, NY 14269
Canadian: P.O. Box 609, Fort Erie, Ont. L2A 5X3

# LINDA LEWIS

## *Cinderella and the Texas Prince*

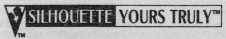

Published by Silhouette Books
**America's Publisher of Contemporary Romance**

For my sister, Candace Jill Grudzien.
Candy, this one's for you, with love.
Thanks for letting me and Cinderella borrow your
close encounter with a cactus.

 **SILHOUETTE BOOKS**

ISBN 0-373-52070-0

CINDERELLA AND THE TEXAS PRINCE

Copyright © 1998 by Linda Kay West

**Printed in U.S.A.**

# About the author

I have always loved stories that begin with "once upon a time" and end with "and they lived happily ever after." You can imagine my delight when my editor suggested that I try a Cinderella story. Making up my own versions of the fairy godmother and the handsome prince was fun, but I have to admit the wicked stepsisters were my favorite creations. I'm not sure what that says about me. Hopefully, only that even good girls like to be bad now and then.

I've always been a very good girl.

Well, there was that one time when I… But that's another story.

This is my fourth book, but my first for Silhouette Yours Truly. The story is about a Louisiana Cinderella who meets her prince in south Texas. On a ranch. I got the inspiration for the setting from my cousins, Bill Martin and Nancy Frasier, who actually have a ranch near Carrizo Springs, Texas, and who generously let me visit from time to time.

Enjoy!

*Linda Lewis*

**Books by Linda Lewis**

**Silhouette Yours Truly**

*Cinderella and the Texas Prince*

**Silhouette Romance**

*Honeymoon Suite* #1113
*The Husband Hunt* #1135
*Cowboy Seeks Perfect Wife* #1226

# *Prologue*

"Sugar, I'm getting the tingle." Mrs. Fae Rae Beneficent, owner and proprietor of At Your Service, an employment agency for butlers, nannies, housekeepers and maids, held a letter in her hand and stared fixedly at the urn.

Her beloved husband, Benny Beneficent, or what was left of his earthly remains, currently resided in a marble urn on top of the oak file cabinet in the corner of her office. Continuing to gaze at the urn, Fae Rae said softly, "I don't like to question your judgment, sweetie pie, but are you sure about this one? I would think the last thing Cindy needs is to be all alone on an isolated ranch."

She glanced at the letter. Did he know exactly what the letter requested? Fae Rae was a little vague about how Benny acquired information these days. "You do realize that the Monarch Ranch needs a housekeeper—more of a caretaker, really—and not a nanny? Cindy has only worked as a nanny. She came to us straight from the orphanage five years ago, remember? A very good nanny she is, too, although the Frerets never appreciated her. The nerve of those people, accusing a sweet, honest girl like Cindy El-

lerbee of…that. As if anyone At Your Service recommended would ever…''

Fae Rae dabbed at the corners of her eyes with a
lace-trimmed hankie and shook her head. ''I really
cannot bring myself to repeat the terrible things those
Frerets said about her. Poor darling. You are right
about one thing, though, Benny, dear. Cindy needs
love, not to mention a family of her very own. But
you can't think she'll find Prince Charming in the
middle of nowhere. No, dear, I'm afraid she'll only
withdraw even more and—''

The tingle escalated to a twitch.

''All right. All right. Settle down now. You know
what's best,'' she said soothingly. Benny had never
liked having his judgment questioned—his tendency
to be bossy had led to many a spectacular argument,
invariably followed by an even more spectacular rec-
onciliation. A wistful smile touched Fae Rae's lips as
she remembered their glorious times together.

Nostalgia kept her from mentioning all those times
in the past when Benny had most assuredly been
*wrong*. She could have reminded him that he was the
one who'd placed Cindy with the Frerets, for example. But he'd been alive then, and subject to human
weaknesses. Benny had been right for the past three
years, ever since he'd gone on to the great beyond.
A man with angelic assistance, spiritual guidance, or
whatever helped him now that she couldn't, ought to
know what he was doing—and what she should do.
Fae Rae got up, walked to the file cabinet and patted
the urn.

The tingle in her fingers and toes subsided. Returning to her desk, Fae Rae picked up the letter she'd
been holding when she got Benny's signal. She reread

it. The letter requested At Your Service to engage a housekeeper for the Monarch Ranch in South Texas. The pay was excellent, the duties light. No one lived at the ranch house. On rare occasions the owners, the fabulously wealthy Rule family, used their old home for entertaining friends and business associates.

Fae Rae pursed her lips. The Rules had a son, didn't they? Two sons, now that she thought about it. If memory served, both in their thirties and both single. She beamed a smile at the urn. "I see your point, Benny dear. What was I thinking? I never ought to have questioned your judgment."

She pressed the buzzer on the intercom. "Mary, dear, would you send in Ms. Ellerbee, please?"

## 1

"**T**ell anyone where I am or what I'm doing, and you're dead meat." Travis Rule unfastened his seat belt and stared balefully at his younger brother.

Treat cut the engine of the Cessna and slanted a teasing glance at Travis. "Aw, shucks. Why can't I spread the word? Afraid the tabloids would come up with another title for you? Like Momma's Boy?"

"That might be better than The Richest Bachelor in Texas. No woman would want a man still tied to his mother's apron strings."

"You're wrong about that, bro. I don't see it myself, but you've got something that draws women to you like bees to nectar."

"Yeah. Money. And a mother hell-bent on getting me married before next week."

"She has her reasons."

Travis snorted. "My impending birthday is no reason to get married."

"Tell that to dear old Mom." In a falsetto voice, Treat continued, "For generations, every male in the Rule family has gotten married before his thirty-fifth birthday, or he hasn't married at all. Travis, dear, have you met Miss X? She's perfect for you."

"Stuff it," snarled Travis. He'd been dodging marriage-minded women for over a year, and the thought of evading two more before he could settle down to running RuleCo had him acting a trifle curmudgeonly.

Treat socked Travis on the shoulder. "Sure thing, bro. But if that's how you feel, why are we here?"

"Think about it," Travis said dryly, reaching for his leather duffel bag.

"Hmm. Mom did come up with some weird plans to get you hitched before the big day. My personal favorite was the contest. Remember that one? 'Tell us in twenty-five words or less why you want to marry Travis Rule, The Richest Bachelor in Texas.' Don't forget, Mom was going to let you choose the winning essay."

Travis shuddered. "After that idea, spending a few days at the ranch with Brooke and Stephanie seems almost sane. And being at the ranch has another great advantage—no media within a hundred miles."

"No *one* within a hundred miles." It was Treat's turn to shudder. "Why did you decide to come early?"

"I want to make sure the new fax modem I had installed in the computer at the ranch house is set up and ready to go. I need it to keep in touch with the office."

Treat sighed. "I keep telling you, bro. All work and no play…"

"Don't start. If you'd quit pretending to be a playboy and get married, Mom might leave me alone, birthday or no birthday."

"Who's pretending? Besides, you're the oldest. It's your duty as First Son to marry and sire an heir to the family fortune."

"Bull. I've done my part for the family fortune—

I quadrupled it.'' Travis eyed his younger brother.
''I've got an idea. Why don't you stay at the ranch
this week? I'll double your salary if you marry
Brooke or Stephanie.''

''They'd never settle for me. Besides, they're your
type, not mine.''

''I don't have a type.''

''The hell you don't. Every woman you've ever
dated, including Brooke and Stephanie, has been petite, blond and beautiful. And rich. You never give
poor girls a second look. It's your fortune-hunter phobia. You want to be loved for yourself, not for your
bankbook, am I right?''

''None of your business.'' Treat was right, as far
as he'd gone. But there was more to his phobia than
that. Travis wanted to avoid being married for his
money, but he had another reason for putting off marriage.

Travis wanted to be in love with the woman he
married.

He couldn't tell his brother that, not unless he
wanted to be subjected to Treat's merciless teasing
for a decade or two. It did make him sound like a
romantic wimp. Conventional wisdom—male wisdom—had it that ''love'' was a woman thing, not
something a grown man wasted time thinking about.
But he'd been giving love a lot of thought lately.

Love existed. Travis could not deny that, and neither could Treat, if he thought about it. They had
grown up with the proof—their mother and father.
But, after waiting years for lightning to strike, bells
to ring, or whatever happened to let a man know his
woman had come along, hope was fading. After four-
teen or fifteen years looking for Miss Right, he hadn't

found her. He had to fact up to it—maybe he never would. The possibility existed that true love might not be for everyone, only for the lucky few.

And it could be that he'd used up his share of the Rule luck on business. Travis had a definite talent for making money. When his father had taken an early retirement—to enjoy time with the love of his life— it had taken Travis only a few years to expand the Rule Company from a sleepy little ranching and mining corporation to a multinational conglomerate. RuleCo now owned banks, insurance companies and the Monarch Hotel chain, as well as ranches, mines and oil and gas wells.

Treat interrupted his brooding with a triumphant hoot.

"I've got an idea. Use Mom's contest idea, but expand on it. Make Stephanie and Brooke compete for your hand."

"What are you talking about?"

"Well, that is the purpose of this trip, isn't it? For you to get to know them better, so you can choose which one to marry?"

"That's Mom's version of their visit, not mine."

"But you're going along with it. Take it one step further, and have some fun while you're at it. Instead of an essay, have them demonstrate how they'd perform their wifely duties."

"Wifely duties?"

"You know. Cooking. Cleaning. Sex."

"That's sick."

"You're sick, if you don't take advantage of the situation. Aren't you attracted to Brooke and Stephanie? They both seem to have the right equipment to turn you on."

"How would you know? Anything in a skirt turns you on."

"I beg your pardon. I have standards. Low ones, I admit, but both Mom's babes are over the top of my scale."

"Then you marry them."

"Nope." Treat gave his brother an exaggerated leer. "Take my advice. Give the final test in the bedroom. The woman with the highest score gets you and Great-Grandmother Rule's engagement ring."

"Shut up and take off. I want to be alone."

"You'll be plenty alone here. At least until Mom and the brides-to-be show up in a day or two. Say, bro. If you don't want to have a contest, you could toss a coin. Or marry both of them. See ya." With another cheeky grin and a wave, Treat revved up the engine and taxied down the runway.

Travis watched as the plane took off and disappeared into the blue South Texas sky. He reached for his cell phone, then remembered he'd purposely left it behind in San Antonio. The tabloids were not above monitoring cellular phone calls. With a shrug, Travis picked up his bag and headed for the small building at the edge of the Monarch Ranch airstrip.

Manuel Ortega, the ranch manager, answered his telephone call.

"Manuel. Travis here. I'm at the strip. Send someone to get me, will you?"

"I'll be there right away, boss," said Manuel.

A few minutes later, Manuel arrived in a black pickup with the Monarch Ranch brand, a royal crown, emblazoned on the doors. He took the leather duffel bag from Travis and pitched it into the back of the truck. "Someone must have slipped up. We weren't expecting you today. If we'd known you were coming, I would have been waiting.''

Sliding into the passenger seat, Travis shut the door. "I decided at the last minute to come a few days early. And I don't want anyone to know I'm here, understand?''

"Not even family?''

"They know. So do a few people at RuleCo. But that's all. I'm trying to avoid the press. Any more stories about me and Mom's marriage frenzy, and my reputation as an astute businessman will never recover.''

"Okay, boss. Whatever you say.''

Thirty minutes later, Manuel brought the pickup to a halt in front of the ranch house. The familiar stucco walls and red-tiled roof never looked more inviting. He needed some time alone in this place. Time to consider his options, map out a strategy for the rest of his life. Should he give up on marriage altogether? Wait a few more years for the right woman to come along? It might be smart to forget about love. There were other reasons to get married.

Travis got out of the pickup, retrieved his bag from the truck bed and entered the house, still contemplating his options. A wife, even one he didn't love, could be an asset. He'd have a hostess for those social occasions company business demanded. He'd have a companion to discuss the many and varied decisions he had to make every day. A mother for his children. Maybe he should give Brooke and Stephanie more than a cursory look.

On the other hand, he could proceed with his original plan. Keep all eligible females at arm's length until he was safely past his thirty-fifth birthday. Then his mother, a firm believer in the family tradition, would leave him to his bachelorhood, positive her oldest son was doomed to live out his life alone. Travis grinned evilly. Then she would turn her attention to Treat.

He was halfway up the stairs before he realized he was not alone. Someone was singing an old Beatles tune. Off-key, loud and a cappella. Setting his bag on the landing, he retreated downstairs and followed the sound to the library. He came to an abrupt halt in the open doorway.

The singer had great legs. Travis couldn't help but notice, since the legs in question were at eye level and bare. His gaze followed their shapely length up to a heart-shaped bottom covered by faded denim cutoffs. The cute little bottom was swaying to and fro, more or less in time to the bad singing.

Vaguely aware that his heart was beating faster than usual, Travis let his gaze drift slowly upward. The vocalist was standing halfway up the library ladder, languidly flicking a feather duster over the shelves as she warbled about yesterdays. She was wearing a Walkman. Hair like black silk hung down her back, almost to her waist. Her back was to him, so he couldn't see her face.

Who in hell was she?

Travis cleared his suddenly dry throat. "Ma'am?" he said, touching her bare ankle.

With a shriek, the woman jerked her foot away from his hand and off the rung of the ladder. Unbalanced, she toppled straight into his arms.

And quite an armful she was. Her silky black hair smelled like roses, and her wide eyes were a smoky shade of gray. Long, sooty eyelashes fluttered. Pink, the same shade as her T-shirt, blossomed beneath elegant cheekbones. "Let me go," she ordered, shoving at his shoulders with both hands. Her husky voice drew his gaze to her mouth. Sexy mouth, full bottom lip, bow-shaped upper.

Suddenly dizzy, he shook his head to clear it. He couldn't be hearing what he thought he was hearing—a choir singing hallelujah! And his fingers and toes were tingling in an alarming fashion. He tightened his hold on his armful and lowered his head to hers.

"I said, put me down! Now!" She turned her head away and wriggled in his arms, all soft curves and sweet smells. Sexy woman.

*His woman.*

Where had that come from? Travis let her go abruptly, backing away from her. "Who are you?"

"What?" she shouted.

He removed the earphones from her ears, brushing her cheek as he did so. Her skin was like silk, too, he thought as he jerked his hand back. "Who are you?" he repeated.

"Cindy Ellerbee. Your housekeeper."

"Excuse me?"

"At Your Service, Mr. Rule, remember? I'm your servant."

*Servant?* This…woman was at his service? A fantasy-making idea if he ever heard one. Him, ruler of the kingdom. Her, his obedient servant. Compelled to do anything he asked of her. For starters, he'd order her to—

She'd called him Mr. Rule. He narrowed his eyes. "How did you know who I was?"

"The painting over the fireplace...the photos everywhere. You and your brother..."

"All right, Mrs. Ellerbee—"

"Miss. I didn't know you were coming."

"*Miss* Ellerbee. I didn't tell anyone I was coming. I'll be here for a few days. Maybe longer. Other guests will be arriving later this week."

"Oh. How many?"

"Three. My mother and two...others." He cleared his throat. "I don't want anyone to know I'm here, so if anyone calls for me, say I'm not here. Or let the machine pick up."

"All right." She eyed him curiously. "The telephone hasn't rung in six months, unless Gus or Manuel were calling."

"I haven't been here. There will be other calls now. Take my word for it."

"I will. If you'll excuse me, I'll get your room ready for you."

"Mine is the one to the left of the stairs, in the front."

"I know." Pink stained her cheeks again. She sidled past him, toward the door. "I'll take care of it, as soon as I change. Wait right here."

"Change? Change what?"

"Clothes. I'm not in uniform."

"You have a uniform?" Visions of French maids began to dance in his head. "Uh, that's not necessary. You look fine. And there's no need to hurry," he called after her. "I'm not ready for bed yet."

She paid no attention, disappearing down the hall leading to the kitchen and the housekeeper's quarters. Travis started to follow her, then changed his mind. He'd take his bag to his room and unpack.

And come to his senses.

No matter what romantic drivel he'd been thinking earlier, he did not believe in love at first sight. There had to be another explanation for his palpitating heart, sweaty palms and panicky feeling. An adrenaline rush, brought on by finding a stranger in the house—that would explain it. As for the angelic chorus, he must have imagined that.

No sensible man falls in love with a stranger, not even one as appealing as Cindy Ellerbee.

He was staring at his bed when Cindy arrived carrying an armful of fresh linens. She had changed. No more cutoffs and T-shirt. No French maid's uniform, either. She was wearing a gray dress, long-sleeved and shapeless, with white collar and cuffs. She'd twisted her hair into a bun at the nape of her neck. If she thought that the dress and old-maid's hairdo made her unattractive, she was sadly mistaken.

"Someone's been sleeping in my bed."

She blushed, bright red this time. "I'm so sorry. If I'd known you were coming..."

"Why were you sleeping in my room? Isn't the housekeeper's suite comfortable?"

"Very comfortable." Her gaze slid away from his. "I've slept in every bed in the house. I don't know why, exactly. Maybe because I could. Being alone in the house, and all." She looked him in the eyes. "I won't do it again."

"No problem." What was going on? This gorgeous woman was not his idea of a housekeeper. And why had she been sleeping in his bed? What if he'd arrived in the morning, early enough to find her there? What if she slept in the nude? What if—

She began stripping the bed, ending his lecherous fantasizing.

"Let me help." Travis tugged the bottom sheet free. He held it to his nose. "Smells like flowers. Your perfume?"

"Lavender. I made lavender sachets for the linen closet. If you don't like the smell—"

"Oh, I like it. But it's more than lavender." He sniffed again. "It smells like…you."

She turned pink again. "I really am sorry I slept in your bed."

"Don't worry about it. Who hired you?"

The change of subject obviously startled her. "You did."

Shaking his head, Travis took the pillow from her and stuffed it into a pillowcase. "My mother was the one who thought we needed someone taking care of the home place. She had me write every agency in San Antonio, Dallas and Houston."

"And New Orleans. At Your Service."

"At my service? That's the second time you've made that offer. How would you like to—"

"At Your Service is the name of the employment agency that sent me here."

"I don't remember writing an agency in New Orleans. How would my mother have known about it?"

"The agency is very well-known among people who need household help. At Your Service places butlers, cooks, maids and housekeepers. And nannies."

"You don't look like any servant I've ever seen."

She nodded. "Because I was out of uniform. But you weren't expected—"

"I don't believe you're a housekeeper."

Frowning, Cindy shook a pillow out of its case. "Why else would I be keeping house?"

"You were waiting for me to show up." Travis slapped his forehead with the heel of his hand. "Mom set this up, didn't she? I should have known she'd have more than one way to keep the family tradition alive."

"Set what up?" Clutching the pillow to her chest, Cindy backed away from the bed. "I don't know what you're talking about."

"You. Me. Alone together. Tell the truth, Ms. Ellerbee." He paused, caught by a sudden thought. "That can't be your real name. Cindyellerbee. Cindyeller. Cinderella. I know Mom's a big fan of fairy tales, but that's a bit obvious, isn't it?"

She dropped the pillow onto the stripped mattress and put her hands on her hips. "You're being offensive, Mr. Rule. And you're not making any sense."

Travis walked around the bed and stood next to her. "I'll spell it out for you. You're here for one reason and one reason only—to get me to propose."

"Propose what?"

"Marriage."

Her hands dropped to her sides. "That's preposterous."

"Why?"

"Why? Why? For starters, I don't want to marry anyone. Ever. Even if I did, why on earth would I want to marry you?"

"You know I'm The Richest Bachelor in Texas. Everyone knows that."

"I didn't." Her eyebrows shot upward. "The very richest?"

"According to the *Dallas Tribune.* They did a story

on the state's most eligible bachelors. Between that and my mother... Never mind. If they hadn't limited the list to bachelors, I would have come in second. Jake Logan is the richest man in the state, but he's already married.'' Travis moved closer, crowding Cindy into the corner of the room. ''Now we've established why you'd want to marry me. But, aside from the obvious lure of the packaging, why would Mom pick you for me?'' Gritting his teeth, Travis ignored the choir humming ominously in the background and insisted, ''You're not my type.''

She swiped her forehead with the back of her hand. ''What a relief! You're not my type, either. I prefer men who are sane. You're crazy!''

''Quite possibly. My family is driving me nuts. Especially my mother.'' He picked up a pillow and fluffed it, letting his gaze drift over his so-called housekeeper. ''Mom must be trying for a little variety. She's got two rich blondes lined up and on the way here. You're not blond, and since you're working for a living, chances are you're not rich, either. I know my mother, though. She's become something of a snob ever since she joined the Daughters of the Texas Revolution. Your family must be well-bred but living in genteel poverty. Ready to sacrifice their daughter on the altar of nouveau riche to restore the family fortune? Am I right?''

Her face, so expressive before, froze. ''Not even close.''

''So tell me what part I got wrong.''

''All of it. I have no family.''

''What?''

''I have no mother, no father, no siblings. Not even a distant cousin, for all I know. I'm an orphan, Mr.

Rule. Now, if you'll excuse me, I'll finish making your bed.''

Mumbling an apology, Travis left Cindy alone in his bedroom. Mentally, he kicked himself all the way down the stairs and out the front door. Cindy Ellerbee, the only woman for whom he'd ever felt...a strong-and-compelling-attraction-at-first-sight, had to think he was a callous, unfeeling jerk. He'd teased her to make her blush that appealing shade of pink—but why had he chosen to tease an orphan about family? He *was* a callous, unfeeling jerk.

Why was she here? If his mother hadn't planted her, and he now recalled that he'd signed the letter offering her the position, why had she applied for the job in the first place? A young—she couldn't be over twenty-three or four—beautiful woman voluntarily choosing to bury herself on an isolated ranch in South Texas did not make sense. He made a mental note to call his office and have her résumé forwarded to him. He needed to know more about her.

He wasn't sure why.

Not because she was Miss Right and he'd fallen in love with her at first sight. That was a fantasy as much as French maids and wolfish lords of the manor. No, he only wanted information about Cindy for business reasons.

He always made it a point to know about his employees.

# 2

A snake had invaded her private paradise.

A snake named Travis Rule. The problem was, this serpent owned the paradise. Grinding her teeth in frustration, Cindy punched the pillow into submission and stuffed it into a pillowcase. He had accused her, flat-out, of being a fortune hunter. How dare he! Of all the arrogant, patronizing, conceited—

He'd thought she'd been lying in wait for him like a…black widow spider. Just like Mercedes Freret—accusing her of weaving a web to entangle Etienne. She was not an insect! Or a man trap.

Or a character in a fairy tale.

Cindyeller he'd called her. Only an insensitive clod would make fun of a person's name. Her name was the only thing her parents had left her, and she was proud to bear it. Regardless of her name, she was no Goody Two-shoes, waiting patiently for some man to come along and rescue her from a life of drudgery.

Hah! As if Mr. Travis Full-of-Himself Rule was her idea of Prince Charming. No self-centered, spoiled rich man would ever appeal to her. She'd had her fill of that kind of man. No matter what he thought, she was not a gold digger, and she was not a drudge. She might be a caretaker, a housekeeper, a servant—strike that. An employee. *His* employee, but she had not and never would sit in the ashes and yearn for the likes of him.

"I ought to quit. I will quit!" Cindy yanked the bedspread up and tucked it around the pillows. "I found one job without references. I can find another. Fae Rae will help. I don't need to work for an unfeeling clod!"

But she'd never find another job that paid so well.

A few more months and she'd have enough money to realize her dream. Then she'd never have to work for anyone else ever again.

Cindy planned to take her savings and open a needlework shop. She'd make it a success, too. She knew everything there was to know about needlepoint, counted cross-stitch, knitting and crocheting. Thanks to Gladys and Mable Hufstatler, she even knew how to tat.

The two spinster sisters who founded the Hufstatler Home for Girls had believed in the old saying, "Idle hands are the devil's workshop." They made sure their wards' hands were always busy, if not with dusting and sweeping or cooking and canning, then with knitting needles and embroidery hoops.

Her shop would be a reality much sooner if she could stay on at the Monarch Ranch for a few more months. If she kept her goal firmly in mind, she could put up with having her employer on the premises for a few days. It was his ranch, after all, no matter how much she'd come to treat it as her own. She'd had six months without anyone around, more time to herself than she'd ever had before.

She loved living alone.

Before her sojourn at the Monarch Ranch, Cindy

had never lived alone. Being smack-dab in the middle of one hundred thousand acres was about as alone as a person could get. At first the sheer size of the ranch had made her uneasy. Not to mention the quiet. The absence of sound had been almost frightening to a city girl. Her former employers had lived in a Victorian mansion on St. Charles Avenue in New Orleans. City noises were always in the background— the rumble of streetcars, the shrill scream of sirens.

She had gotten used to the quiet. And, while she was the only occupant of the ranch house, she'd never been completely alone in the middle of all those acres. The ranch manager, Manuel Ortega, or his wife, Dolores, checked on her once or twice a week. Their house was several miles away, closer to the main entrance to the ranch. And one or the other of the cowboys—there were three of them—might drop in now and then, usually on days when she'd baked cookies or cakes. Gus Griswald, the bunkhouse cook, limited his dessert making to pies.

Cindy did not relish the idea of being alone with Travis Rule, but she could do it. It wouldn't be for long. A few days, he'd said. And other people were on the way, one of them his mother. Mrs. Rule would tell him she had not been "planted" on the premises to entice him into proposing marriage. What a colossal ego the man had!

She would have continued finding fault with Travis Rule, but a tweak from her pesky conscience prodded her to review her own behavior.

Smoothing the last wrinkle out of the bedspread, Cindy replayed her encounter with Travis. He *had* caught her sleeping in his bed. Her cheeks grew hot. How could she have done such a thing? Never before had she even thought about treating someone else's things as her own.

The months of being alone in the house, without a boss in sight, must have dulled her sense of propriety. She knew her place, and it was not in her employer's bed! No doubt about it, she'd grown lax in her duties—not keeping to a schedule, forgetting to wear a uniform. Sleeping all over the house.

She wouldn't have to quit. He'd fire her. He was probably downstairs now, writing out her final paycheck.

Oh, darn. Even with Fae Rae's help, she would never find another job as good as this one. Not with the Frerets' awful accusations hanging over her head. And she wanted—needed her needlework shop. The shop would be more than a business to her, it would be her place, the place she belonged, where she and no one else would control her destiny.

Maybe if she apologized again...

No! She'd been wrong, but so had he. *Sneaking* up on her with no advance warning. He probably enjoyed catching his employees off guard. At least he'd caught her working. What if he'd come one of the days when she'd worked all night and slept all day? Then he'd have had more reason to fire her.

Cindy sat on the edge of the bed and chewed on her bottom lip. Maybe he would overlook her transgressions. They weren't so very bad. And she'd already said she was sorry. Twice. He'd only apologized once, and not for catching her off guard, only for assuming she had a family. Not that he'd needed to apologize for that. He couldn't have known she was an orphan.

He hadn't apologized for being cocky and conceited. He probably didn't even acknowledge that he had those faults. But what else would you call a man who assumed every woman he came in contact with wanted to marry him?

Grudgingly, Cindy had to concede that Travis might have a reason or two to jump to that conclusion. Some women might admire toast brown hair, especially the wayward strand that flopped onto his forehead now and then. Sky blue eyes that gleamed with mischief might appeal to a woman or two, she supposed. An unscientific survey might reveal that a majority of females would find his tall frame, broad shoulders and hard body attractive. Most women wouldn't fault him for being rich, either.

She would. She had no use for Travis Rule and his money.

Except on payday.

Tucking a strand of hair back in place, Cindy decided her chances of getting another few month's wages from her employer were good. Travis wouldn't fire her. According to Fae Rae, it had taken months for the Rule family to fill the caretaker-housekeeper position this time. More to the point, Prince Uncharming didn't look like the type who could take care of himself.

He needed her as much as she needed the job.

Cindy knew just how she would deal with him. From now on, she would be professional and polite. And distant. She would overlook the teasing gleam in his blue eyes, and she would completely ignore his handsome face, all angles and planes except for a mouth that curved easily into a grin.

She really did know her place, and from now on she'd stay firmly there. And she would move on when she was ready, not before. Certainly not because of *him*.

Picking up the sheets, Cindy walked briskly out the bedroom door. She collided head-on with Travis as she turned into the hallway. He grabbed her by the elbows as she staggered backward.

"Sorry. I didn't mean to run you over." He steadied her, moving his hands from her arms to her waist.

"My fault. I couldn't see over the linens. You can let me go now." She kept her voice steady and cool, even though for some inexplicable reason her pulse was racing.

"Sure you're all right?" He dropped his hands, but moved closer.

Cindy quickly backed away, bumping against the wall. Clutching her load of laundry, she replied, "I'm fine. I'm usually not this clumsy."

"You probably don't usually have men trying to knock you down."

"No, I don't," she snapped. "How long do you plan to stay?"

One eyebrow quirked upward. "A few days. At least until my birthday. Is that a problem?"

Cindy bit her tongue. Tact, try a little tact, she told herself. The object was to be professional, not insolent. "No, of course not. So you'll be here until around August fifth?"

"How did you know my birth date?"

Ducking her head, she mumbled, "I read your baby book."

"My baby book?" He sounded startled. And pleased.

Travis probably thought she'd been mooning over his baby pictures for months. "I looked at Treat's—

your brother's—too," she said. "They were on the table in the library, along with the photo albums and scrapbooks. I didn't think they were meant to be private."

"Don't get prickly, Cindy. Mom's a big one on showing off the family. She'd be thrilled that you took an interest."

"Oh. Well, then. If you'll excuse me, I'll take these to the laundry room. When will you be wanting dinner?"

He followed her down the stairs. "I don't care. Six, seven. What time do you eat?"

"It varies. I'll have dinner ready at half past six, if that's all right."

"Fine."

She stopped at the bottom of the stairs, shifting the load of laundry to one hip. "Is there anything you don't like?"

"I don't like it when you look at the floor when you talk to me."

Stubbornly she kept her eyes focused on the toes of her sensible black pumps. "I meant food. Are there any foods you don't like?"

"Beets," he said, using one finger to tilt her chin upward. "I hate beets. And liver. Never did care for liver. Do you have to wear that dress?"

"Excuse me?" She looked him straight in the eye. Disapprovingly. He didn't appear to notice.

"That dress. It looks hot. Long sleeves and a high neck are not right for South Texas in July. If you want to wear shorts, I don't mind."

"The house is air-conditioned," she reminded him.

"Nevertheless, you look hot." He stepped closer. "Come to think of it, I feel a little warm myself.

Maybe it's not the dress, after all. And maybe I did hear…''

He had her backed against the wall again. ''I'm not hot, not at all,'' she insisted, lowering her eyes again. Looking into his blue ones made her feel funny. Dizzy. Weak.

''You're glowing.'' He ran a finger across her brow, making her aware of the moisture there.

''Glowing?'' She peeked at him through her lashes.

''My mother always said that horses sweat, men perspire and women glow. You're glowing. So you are hot.''

''Mr. Rule, please—''

''Call me Travis. If you've memorized my baby book, you know me well enough to use my first name.''

''I haven't memorized it! I merely glanced at it. Once. Now, if you'll excuse me—''

He touched her hair. ''And you don't have to put your hair up like that. Don't all those hairpins give you a headache?''

They did, but she wasn't about to admit it to him.

Travis—Mr. Rule was acting less and less like an employer. How could she remain distant and aloof when he insisted on hovering over her like this? ''No, they don't. Let me by, please.''

He stepped back, almost wresting the sheets away from her as he did. ''I'll do the laundry while you fix dinner.''

She held on to her load of sheets. ''That won't be necessary.''

''You don't want my help?''

''No. I definitely do not want your help. I am perfectly capable of doing my job without assistance.''

"I believe you. No need for you to get testy." He stopped tugging on the sheets and backed away from her.

Cindy hurried down the hall, well aware that Travis was only a step or two behind her. She walked through the spacious kitchen to the laundry room. Placing the sheets and pillowcases in the washer, she added detergent and turned on the machine. Then she returned to the kitchen.

Travis was seated at the oak table in the bay window, gazing out at the kitchen patio. Except for a wrought iron bench, the small area enclosed by a low adobe wall had been bare when she arrived.

"You've made some changes," he said.

"I planted a few herbs, that's all." Travis was not behaving in character. She'd read enough about him in the scrapbooks memorializing his rapid rise in the business world to know that. A grown man, CEO of his family's international consortium of companies, should have better things to do than sit around watching herbs grow.

"It looks nice. All those hanging baskets and terracotta pots filled with greenery. Did you grow the lavender you used to make the sheets smell good?"

"Yes. I'm going to cook dinner now." So why don't you go away? According to *Barron's,* Travis Rule could read a person's body language like a book—one of the secrets of his phenomenal success. Cindy concentrated on making every inch of her body tell him to leave.

He leaned back in the chair, turning his gaze from the patio to her. "Fine. I'll watch. What are we having?"

"Jambalaya." She tied an apron around her waist

and got out the stockpot. What had Miss Hufstatler told her time and again? Never believe anything you read, and only half of what you see. She'd never trust a financial magazine again.

"Don't you need seafood for that? Not much seafood around here, except for catfish."

"Chicken and sausage jambalaya." Cindy got a green pepper and celery from the refrigerator and placed them on the counter next to the food processor. She walked to the pantry and selected a large onion and several cloves of garlic. She glanced at the clock on the wall. It was a little after four, and the spicy mix would need an hour or so to cook. Time was not a problem, but her audience was making her jumpy. "This will take a while. If you're hungry, I could serve you a snack in the family room. Or in your office." The farther away, the better.

"I can wait. You don't mind if I watch, do you?"

"As a matter of fact—"

"Better yet, I could help with the chopping." He got up from the table and came to stand beside her at the counter.

The man had not gotten the message. How dense did that make him? Hadn't she told him she could do her job by herself? "That won't be necessary. The food processor will do the chopping." Cindy shoved the celery into the feed tube and turned on the machine.

Travis retreated to his chair. "Independent little thing, aren't you?"

"Yes, to the 'independent.' But I'm not exactly 'little.'" Cindy stood five feet seven inches tall in her bare feet. She still had to look up at him. He had to be at least half a foot taller than she was.

"No, I guess you're not the petite type, are you?"

Out of the corner of her eye, she saw his eyebrows snap together in a confused frown. What was that about?

"Don't you ever need help?" he asked.

She started to shake her head, but an image of Fae Rae's concerned face forced her to tell the truth. "Of course. But not with cooking."

Once the vegetables were chopped, she put them aside and added oil to the pot. She'd deboned and cubed the chicken and sliced the sausage earlier— chorizo, since Cajun *andouille* was in short supply in South Texas. She sautéed the sausage first, then added the chicken.

Travis watched in silence for a while as she continued with sautéing the meat and vegetables. "Where did you learn to cook jambalaya? Oh, I remember. You're from Louisiana."

"Yes. I was born in New Orleans."

"Great place."

"Yes."

"Did you grow up there?"

"A few miles up-river. The orphanage was in the country, near St. Francisville."

"What happened to your family?"

"They drowned when the ferry they were on collided with an oil tanker and sank."

"How old were you?"

"Eight."

"That must have been tough."

"I survived."

"How did you end up here, in the middle of nowhere."

"I applied for the job, and I got it."

"Obviously. I want to know *why* you applied for the position. Was the ad misleading? Did it promise adventure and excitement?"

"No. It promised a very good wage for very easy work."

"You think taking care of a twelve-room house is easy?"

She added chicken stock and rice and put the lid on the pot before turning to answer him. "There hasn't been anyone around to get it dirty."

"Until I showed up."

"It's your house." Cindy bit her tongue. She was getting snippy again, but Travis and all his questions were beginning to grate on her nerves.

"So it is. You don't strike me as a lazy person. If light duties weren't the appeal of this job, it must have been the money."

"Yes."

"Ah. So you admit you're interested in money?"

"Why shouldn't I admit it? Being paid to do a job isn't something to be ashamed of."

"No, you're right. But there are faster ways to get rich—"

She stopped him with a glare.

"—but you've already said you aren't interested in marrying for money."

"That's right. I'm not."

"And you don't mind being all alone in the middle of nowhere?"

"I adore being alone," she said severely.

Travis winced. "I'll be out of your way soon, Cindy, I promise." He got up and moved to the stove. "That smells good already. But aren't you making too much for just the two of us?"

"I had planned to take the ingredients to the bunk-house and cook it for Gus and the boys." She began wiping off the counters and putting dishes in the dishwasher.

"Grizzly Gus lets you cook for him?"

"We have a deal. I'm teaching him Cajun and he's showing me how to cook Tex-Mex."

"Hmm. That doesn't sound like Gus. I've never known him to let anyone near his stove. You must be a real charmer."

He probably thought she should use a little charm on him. Ha! No way! Polite professionalism was all he was going to get from her. "I don't know about that. Gus and I struck a bargain, that's all."

"You must be a skilled negotiator. With that kind of talent, you could be doing something besides keeping house."

She turned on the water in the sink full force, hoping to drown him out. It didn't work.

He moved closer and shouted, "Where was your last job?"

She stiffened. "New Orleans."

"You were a housekeeper?"

"Not exactly." Turning off the water, she opened a drawer and took out a tablecloth and napkins and headed for the dining room. "I'll just set the table now. You don't mind if I use the pottery and not the china, do you? As I said before, dinner will be ready at six-thirty. I'll fix a salad to go with the jambalaya. I made bread yesterday, but if you'd prefer hot rolls, I can make those. And there's pecan pie for—"

"Whoa, there. What got you started?"

She shot him a confused look. "What?"

"For a woman of few words, you got awfully talkative all of a sudden. And don't set the table in the dining room. I'd rather eat in the kitchen. With you.''

Cindy stopped. "Very well." She returned the tablecloth to the drawer, and got two place mats instead.

Watching her arrange the table, Travis asked, "What were we talking about? Oh, yeah. Your last job. Why did you leave? Does this job pay so much more than your last job?"

"Yes, it does."

"I'm surprised. I'd have thought the better-paying jobs would be in the city."

"Not for someone without a college education."

"You didn't go to college?" He appeared shocked.

"No. The orphanage taught us the skills they thought we needed to make our way, cooking, sewing, child care—"

"Sounds like they were training you to be wives, not career women."

"These days a lot of career women need someone to take care of their homes and families. The women who run the orphanage figured that out, and so did Fae Rae."

"Fae Rae?"

"Fae Rae Beneficent. She's the owner of At Your Service."

"The employment agency. Sounds like they might be able to find a man a wife, too. The old-fashioned, noncareer kind of wife."

"Is that the kind you want?"

"I don't want any kind of wife at all. But my mother, the matchmaker has other ideas. She expects me to find a wife and get married before I'm thirty-five."

"She gave you a marriage deadline?" Cindy blurted, interested in spite of herself.

"She did, backed up by several generations of Rule ancestors. All the Rule men for generations have married before their thirty-fifth birthday, or they haven't married at all."

"You don't have much time left."

"No." He leaned against the counter and folded his arms across his chest. "Unless I go along with my mother's plan. If I do that, I'll be on my honeymoon in a matter of days."

"Is that so?" Cindy went back to the stove and checked the jambalaya. Why wouldn't he go away? She really did not care about Travis and his wedding woes.

"Or I might meet someone who could change my mind about marriage. Even if I did, at this late date I'd have to fall in love at first sight."

"That's not likely, is it?"

"Don't you believe in love at first sight?"

"No." Thanks to Etienne she'd gotten over believing in love at all.

"You didn't feel…anything out of the ordinary when we met, for instance?"

"Only surprise." Cindy stopped stirring the pot and risked looking in his eyes. "Why? You're not saying you felt something, are you?"

His gaze slid away. "No. Of course not. Only surprise, like you said. I wasn't expecting to find anyone here."

"You forgot about hiring a housekeeper?"

"I must have. I've had other things on my mind lately. My mother is doing everything she can to make sure I don't end up a bachelor. She's sure that's what's going to happen if I don't get married before August. She's real big on tradition. The truth is, Cindy, my mother and her matchmaking have made me a little crazy."

"Oh, I see. No wonder you said your mother planted me here. You thought I was part of her plan."

"Exactly."

"But your mother isn't matchmaking with me—she doesn't even know me."

"You don't know my mother. If she'd known about you, she definitely would have used you. She's relentless, and a little desperate. Not only because she's big on family tradition—she wants grandchildren. The sooner, the better." He made a noise halfway between a sigh and a groan. "Mom's been throwing potential brides at me every chance she gets. It's not easy avoiding single ladies, you know. Even way out here in the middle of nowhere. I walk into what I thought would be the safest place on the planet, at least for a day or two, and look what I found. You." That teasing grin was back.

Cindy half rose from her chair. "I never threw myself at you."

"Not intentionally, I know. But you did fall into my arms."

"Only because you startled me." She got up and walked to the stove.

"I know. But something happened to me when I held you. I need to figure out exactly what..." He stopped and looked out the window. "You didn't hear...music when you were in my arms, did you?"

"Yes, I did."

His blue eyes flashed, and that grin appeared again. "You did? What did it sound like?"

She narrowed her eyes. "The Beatles."

"No." The grin faded away. "I was thinking of another kind of music." He ducked his head and mumbled, "Maybe an angelic choir singing hallelujah?"

"Certainly not."

"You're sure?"

"I don't know what you're talking about."

"Neither do I," he muttered.

"What?"

"If it wasn't mutual, it doesn't matter. I must have imagined…"

"Imagined what? That I fell into your arms on purpose?"

"Something like that. Anyway, reflexes took over, and I—"

"Reflexes? Your assumption that every woman you meet wants to marry you is automatic?"

"Something like that. I know it sounds immodest, but believe me, Cindy, most women I meet do want to marry me. Hell, as far as I can tell, they all do. The money, you know."

"The Richest Man in Texas."

"Bachelor. The Richest Bachelor in Texas. It's a curse. But with all those other women, I never heard— There's got to be a way to find out—" He snapped his fingers. "Of course. Kiss me, Cindy."

He reached for her, and she almost let those tempting lips touch hers before she came to her senses and reacted.

She popped him on the nose with the wooden spoon.

His eyes watering, Travis rubbed his nose. "Ouch. Why did you do that?"

"Why did you try to kiss me?"

"I wanted to see if I'd hear—" He shoved his hands in his pockets. "Hell, I don't know. It seemed like a good idea at the time."

"Well, it wasn't! I don't want to kiss you!"

"You don't? Are you sure? I've been told I do it very well."

"Read my lips, Mr. Rule—I don't care! What is your problem? You're not acting like a shrewd, sensible businessman, *Time Magazine*'s Entrepreneur of the Year. You're not even acting your age!" She waved the wooden spoon under his nose. "You, Mr. Rule, are behaving like a jerk!"

He dodged the spoon. "A jerk?"

"A real jerk." She poked him in the chest with the spoon, leaving a red stain on his shirt. "Walking in here unannounced, accusing me of...of being after you for your money. Following me everywhere, never leaving me alone!" She poked him again. "I like being alone! I don't care how much money you've got. I don't want your money. I don't want you. Is that very clear?"

He nodded, looking bewildered and contrite. And younger than thirty-four. He looked like a little boy who'd been punished unfairly. Which was not true, because he'd definitely deserved a pop on the nose. "Well, is it?"

"Very clear," he said, his voice low. "I was out of line. I'm sorry."

Mollified, she put down the spoon and picked up a dishcloth. Taking a calming breath, she dampened the cloth. "I got red gravy on your shirt. Let me get it off before the stain sets."

"I'll do it." He took the cloth from her and began

dabbing at the spot. "I am extremely sorry, Cindy. Miss Ellerbee."

"You should be. I need this job. But not enough to put up with your bizarre behavior." Now his face was red—either he was embarrassed or running a fever. "You're not sick, are you?"

"I think maybe I am. In the head. I'm going to lie down for a while." He walked toward the kitchen door. "Call me when dinner is ready. Please."

# 3

When dinner was over, Travis holed up in his office and checked out the fax. He sent a few messages, one requesting a copy of Cindy Ellerbee's résumé, then made an early night of it. After hours of tossing and turning, he gave up trying to sleep and threw his pillow on the floor. The damn thing still smelled like a woman. Not just any woman. A specific, gray-eyed, independent, self-sufficient, prickly woman. Cindy Ellerbee.

*His woman.*

Travis turned on his stomach and put his hands over his ears to block out the choir, in case it decided to burst into song again. Love at first sight? Come on! No sane person believed in that nonsense.

A faint humming noise, like a choir warming up, sounded in his ears.

Travis rolled over and stared at the ceiling. So maybe he wasn't so sane anymore. Something, or someone had driven him over the edge, and now he was nuts.

Or not.

Heart palpitations and strange ringing in the ear didn't necessarily add up to insanity. Or love. More than likely some rare disease caused his symptoms.

And he could make his own diagnosis—brain fever, brought on by the weight of generations pushing him toward the marriage deadline.

He'd see a doctor, get a prescription and be his old self in no time.

That settled, Travis squeezed his eyes shut and tried counting stock options one more time. He had no more success this time than the dozen times he'd tried that trick earlier. Wide awake, he inventoried his bodily systems. His heart was working fine, pounding away. He could move all his extremities. Feet, hands, arms and legs all responded as ordered. Travis proved that by sitting up and feeling his forehead. No fever. He swallowed. No sore throat.

All right. So he wasn't physically sick. That didn't leave mental illness as the only other possible cause of his symptoms. It could be lust. It *had* to be lust. Sexual frustration did strange things to a man. And he had been avoiding women for over a year. Not an easy job. He'd been pursued by a fair number of females ever since puberty.

But after the media had stuck him with The Richest Bachelor in Texas title, women had come at him from every which way. If he'd followed Treat's salacious advice, he would have had a different woman every night. But he hadn't succumbed to temptation.

Except for escorting Brooke or Stephanie to a few charity functions, he'd stayed at home alone every Saturday night since his last birthday. He hadn't wanted to encourage any of the many women throwing themselves at his feet to think she had a chance of becoming Mrs. Travis Rule. He'd been a damn saint.

Retrieving the pillow he'd tossed on the floor, he

put it behind his head and closed his eyes. Sleep still eluded him. He couldn't stop thinking about Cindy.

His woman, ha!

If she was his woman, why hadn't she recognized him as her man? What kind of Cupid only shot arrows into one-half of a couple destined for a marriage-made-in-heaven? Cindy may have fallen into his arms at first sight, but she sure as hell hadn't fallen in love that same instant. No choir had shouted hallelujah! in her ears.

Travis groaned. He had a fever all right. And Cindy Ellerbee was the cause.

And the cure. He knew how to get a woman out of his system. He'd done it a time or two when he'd been young and hormone driven. He'd seen Treat do it on a regular basis since puberty. He needed to make love to her until the fever subsided. And he needed to do it *now,* not two weeks from now.

That could be a problem.

Cindy wouldn't let him near enough to kiss her, much less…

Why couldn't he have been a little more subtle? He'd followed her around like a puppy, getting in her way while she'd tried to work. He'd made crude, suggestive comments more suited to a teenage boy suffering from testosterone poisoning than a responsible, adult male. No wonder she'd been disgusted with him.

He'd always prided himself on the patience and restraint with which he conducted his business affairs. And his other affairs, too, for that matter. What had happened to his vaunted control? He'd grabbed for Cindy like she was his favorite candy bar and he was six years old.

Control. That was the answer. He had to get himself back in control. Once he was himself again—cool and calculating, sane and sensible—Cindy Ellerbee wouldn't stand a chance. She'd fall into his arms, and his bed, like a ripe peach.

Travis threw back the sheet and got out of bed. If he couldn't sleep, he might as well put the time to good use.

Strategy needed to be plotted, tactics decided upon.

But first he needed more facts. The bedside clock glowed the time—5:00 a.m. Gus Griswold would be up and banging pots and pans in the bunkhouse kitchen in a matter of minutes. Travis quickly dressed and tiptoed downstairs in his stocking feet, carrying his boots. He didn't want to wake Cindy.

He didn't want to see her again, not until he had more information about what she liked, what she hated, what she dreamed about. If she'd talked Gus into swapping cooking lessons, the old reprobate had to know more about her than he did. Even the fact she'd made the effort to get past Gus's sharp tongue told him something about her. Grizzly Gus had an image that he worked hard to maintain—that he was tough as cowhide and mean as a rattlesnake. It took a perceptive person to see through his ornery facade. Cindy had to be a good judge of people. And if she'd put up with Gus and his grumbling just so he'd teach her how to make enchiladas, she had to have a real love of learning.

He could think of a few things he wanted to teach her.

Travis stopped long enough to write a note letting Cindy know he was having breakfast at the bunkhouse, then he slipped out the door and went to the

three-car garage attached to the house by a breezeway. He got in the pickup, leaving the Bronco and
the Cadillac for Cindy to use if she needed to go
somewhere before he got back.

The bunkhouse was a couple of miles away, close
to the barns and corrals. When Travis arrived, the
lights on the first floor, which housed the kitchen and
the living room, were blazing.

"Hello, Gus. Boys." He nodded to the three young
cowboys busily stuffing themselves with pancakes,
eggs and sausage.

"Travis?" Gus stopped flipping pancakes long
enough to slap Travis on the shoulder. "Manuel told
us you'd showed up unexpectedlike. What in tarna-
tion are you doing up and about at this time of day?"

"I came for breakfast."

"Well, sit yourself down, son. I'll have a stack of
flapjacks ready before you can whistle 'Deep in the
Heart of Texas.'"

After breakfast Travis waited for the three cowboys
to take their leave. "So, how've you been?" he asked
Gus, not sure how to begin his interrogation. Something was definitely wrong with him—he was never
unsure of himself.

"Tolerable. Tolerable. What are you doing back at
the ranch? Thought you had to keep your nose to the
grindstone, now that you're the biggest man in
Texas."

"Richest, not biggest. The business can take care
of itself for a week or so. I needed to get away for a
while."

"You needed to hide out for a while, more likely.
Where's Sal?"

"Mom will be here in a day or two. She's bringing some people with her."

"Girl people?"

"Yeah," said Travis morosely.

Gus gave him a sly look. "Your birthday's getting close. Reckon your ma is pulling out all the stops, trying to get you hitched before the big day."

"You got that right."

"And you ain't quite ready to get into harness with any little filly."

"Not hardly."

"Not even a prospect in sight?"

Travis shrugged. "Mom's settled on a couple—the two she's bringing to the ranch for a visit."

"How about you? Seems to me a man ought to take a hand in picking out his woman."

*His woman.* "That's who—what I want to talk to you about."

"Me? I ain't running no dating service here. I don't know nothing about female types. And I'm too gosh-darn old to learn."

"You know about one female—Cindy Ellerbee."

Chuckling, Gus scraped the last plate and stuck it in the dishwasher. "Cindy. Ain't she a pretty thing? Good cook, too. She learned me how to cook that there ay-too-fay, and I'm showing her the finer points of chuck-wagon kwezeen."

"She told me."

Gus stopped scrubbing the griddle long enough to slant a suspicious look at Travis. "What's got you interested in that tall drink of water? I thought you liked them little bitty blondes."

He must have really gotten in a rut. Even Gus knew

what kind of woman he usually dated. "I used to. Now I like tall, long-legged brunettes."

"You ain't planning on taking advantage of Cindy, are you?" Gus waved a spatula under Travis's nose in a threatening manner.

"No. I just want to know more about her."

"Why are you so all-fired interested in her?"

"Because. Come on, Gus, give. I need to know about Cindy."

"I'll tell it to you straight, Travis Rule. She's not the gal for you."

"Why not?" What was wrong with him, anyway? First, Cindy, now Gus, who'd known him since he was a baby, thought he wasn't good enough for Cindy Ellerbee. That stung. He'd always thought of himself as having all the qualities needed to attract the opposite sex—he was trustworthy, reliable, honest. He never made promises he didn't keep.

So maybe Treat was the real good-looking guy in the family. Still and all, his face didn't stop clocks or make babies cry. Plus, to continue blowing his own horn, he was successful, rich and he had a sense of humor. Up until now that had made him more than acceptable to any woman he'd met. "Why wouldn't she and I get along?"

"For starters, Cindy wasn't born with a silver spoon in her mouth."

"That much I know. Has she said anything about her life before she came to Monarch Ranch?"

"Nary a word. Cindy don't talk your ear off like a lot of women. She's quiet and refinedlike. Hasn't got a family, you know. Poor little gal had to make her own way in the world. So she's not spoiled rotten, like you and Treat. You two boys had everything handed to you on a silver platter."

"Not everything," Travis muttered. "What else? Does she date much?"

"You planning on asking her out?"

"Yeah, I am."

"I don't think that's a good idea. Cindy's not up to handling a man like you."

Travis rubbed his nose. "She hasn't had any problem so far. Do you know how old she is?"

"Twenty-five. A leetle bit too young for you, come to think of it. You're almost ten years older than her. You got a hankering to seduce and abandon her?" Gus eyed Travis, picking up a butcher knife and rubbing his thumb along the blade.

"None of your business. But I'm not planning on hurting her."

"I know you wouldn't *plan* on it. You always were tenderhearted when it came to strays and orphans and such. But you might do it anyway, accidentallike. Cindy was mighty sad when she first came here. She's perked up considerable since then. Now, most days, she's as frisky as a newborn colt. Wouldn't like to see her unhappy again."

"Neither would I. Did she ever say what was making her sad?"

"Not a peep. Not to me no ways."

"You think she might have opened up to someone else?"

"Mebbe."

"Who? Is she seeing anyone?"

"She sees a few folks. Me. The boys."

"She's not dating one of them, is she?"

"Naw. She's not interested in young fellows still

wet behind the ears. Not that they haven't asked. But she turned 'em down, nice and polite."

"Is she going out with anyone in town?"

"Don't think so. No one from town's been out here lately, 'cept on business. Usual bunch from the Border Patrol cruise in every now and then, but they don't stop at the big house."

"She could be seeing someone in Carrizo Springs or Crystal City, even if they don't come out here."

"No, she couldn't. She never goes to town by herself."

"Why not?"

"She doesn't know how to drive."

"Everyone knows how to drive."

"Not standard shift. And she won't touch the Caddy. She's scared of putting a dent in it. Since she's been here, I drive her into Carrizo Springs or Crystal City every week or so to get groceries. Manuel and Dolores take her to church every Sunday. She's a Methodist."

"I think I'll head over to the Ortegas'." He should have thought of that sooner. A woman would talk to another woman about things she'd never tell a man. The only other female within fifty miles was Dolores Ortega.

Travis said goodbye to Gus, got back in the pickup and took the road that led to the Monarch Ranch main gate. He pulled in the driveway of the white brick ranch house where his ranch manager lived.

Dolores answered the door. "Señor Travis! *Buenas días.* Manuel told me you had come home. Can I get you anything? Coffee?"

"No, thanks. I just had breakfast at the bunkhouse."

"Are you looking for Manuel? He went into Carrizo to talk to that cattle buyer from Fort Worth. He should be back in time for lunch."

"That's okay. I wanted to talk to you."

"Me? What about?"

"Cindy Ellerbee."

A smile wreathed Dolores's face. "Ah, Cindy. She is a very nice girl. And so talented."

"Talented? Oh, you mean her cooking. Is she teaching you how to make *étouffée,* too?"

"Not only her cooking. She's a wonderful seamstress. She knits, she embroiders, she quilts. Not too many girls her age have those kinds of skills nowadays. She donated some beautiful things she'd made to the church bazaar."

"Did she?"

"*Sí.* Cindy is very generous with her time. She is teaching me how to crochet, and I'm teaching her *español.*"

"She barters a lot, doesn't she? I wonder why?"

Dolores shrugged. "Bartering's a friendly way to do business. And Cindy is saving her money."

"What for, do you know?"

"No. All I know is she takes her paycheck to the bank every month and puts most of it in a savings account."

"She doesn't go to town often, or so Gus says."

"She can't. She doesn't know how to drive a standard shift. That's all there is at the ranch house, except for the Cadillac." Dolores paused, an anxious look on her face. "Why all the questions? Is there anything wrong with Cindy?"

"No. Not at all. I'm just curious about her, that's

all. Don't you find it strange that a young woman like her would bury herself on this ranch?''

"Some people like being alone."

"So you think Cindy is a loner?"

Dolores shook her head. ''Not anymore. But, I have to admit, I did at first. She was very quiet, very self-contained. Too tell the truth, I thought she was stuck-up. But that didn't last long. A few trips together to town, and she opened up like a flower. Now I'm sure she was never a snob, only sad and a little shy.''

"Has she said what made her sad?"

"No. And I didn't ask. It's none of my business." The look she gave him let him know she didn't think it was any of his business, either.

"I only asked because I like my employees to be happy," said Travis. "So, let me see the newest Ortega."

Beaming, Dolores led him to the nursery.

Cindy found Travis's note on the kitchen table. Her first reaction was relief. She didn't have to face him quite yet. After the dream she'd had last night... Her subconscious was crazy, weaving dreams around a man like Travis Rule. She should be dreaming about her needlework shop, not him. Shaking her head in dismay, she reached for the coffee canister and measured out enough for a full pot.

Her second thought was that he must not have liked her cooking. Then she remembered—he'd had three helpings of jambalaya. Maybe he'd decided to avoid her because he thought there were too many weapons in the kitchen. She had hit him with the spoon. No telling what she might do with a frying pan. Or a carving knife.

They had just met, after all. Travis couldn't know that she didn't usually resort to violence. She'd never assaulted anyone before. But he had started it. He'd tried to kiss her. What kind of man tried to kiss a woman he'd only just met? An unprincipled womanizer, that's what kind.

Just like Etienne.

Etienne Breaux had been her first love. And she'd sworn he'd be her last. If she'd known more about the male of the species, she never would have fallen in love with Mercedes Freret's younger brother. She would have seen Etienne for what he was—a scoundrel. A charming scoundrel, to be sure, but a scoundrel nevertheless.

As it was, she'd believed every lie Etienne had told her. And what had her love and trust gotten her? A broken heart and a ruined reputation. At least she'd managed to hold on to a scrap of pride. And a smidgen of strength. She'd had just enough backbone to keep her disgrace from sending her into a spiral of despair.

The months alone at the Monarch Ranch had restored both her pride and her spirit. She might not know much about men, but she knew enough to keep Travis Rule right where he belonged—out of her dreams and out of her way. He wasn't even charming, for heaven's sake!

Cindy put the coffee on and went upstairs to clean Travis's room. She would be in and out before he returned from the bunkhouse. Pushing open the door, she was surprised to see that the bed had been neatly made. No clothes were strewn around the room.

Cindy found them in the clothes hamper in the adjoining bathroom. That room was neat, too.

Cindy checked the towels hanging on the rack. They were damp. A brief, but embarrassingly detailed, image of Travis in the shower, naked, flashed through her mind. She ruthlessly suppressed it. Her libido could just give it up. She wasn't about to get in trouble over a man again because of frantic hormonal urges.

Jerking the towels from the rack, she took them and the clothes from the hamper to the laundry room. After she started the washer, Cindy set up the ironing board and plugged in the iron.

Why had Travis gone to see Gus? To find out just how strange his new housekeeper was? Surely Gus would tell him she'd been doing a good job. Gus didn't know that she'd slept in every bed in the house, or that she'd sometimes slept all day and worked at night. But he had seen her in slacks or shorts. Gus could tell Travis she hadn't worn a uniform for months.

Sighing, Cindy pulled one of the shapeless gray dresses out of a basket. She tested the iron and began ironing the dress. One way or another, this job couldn't last much longer.

If Travis didn't fire her for incompetence, she'd have to quit to avoid his unwelcome advances. Unwelcome and inept. She would have expected a man like him to be more sophisticated in his approach. Smoother.

Travis had said women threw themselves at him. That could explain it—he never had to resort to charm to get a woman. He only had to flash his bank book or mention his title. Richest Bachelor in Texas—what a silly claim to fame! A sensible man ought to be embarrassed by such nonsense.

Cindy finished ironing five identical dresses and five crisp, white aprons, then went to take the clothes out of the dryer. Discovering that the shirt Travis had worn yesterday had a tiny rip, Cindy got out her sewing kit. She was embroidering a small crown over the tear when Travis returned.

"Good morning," she said coolly.

"Hello. Gus sends his greetings. So does Dolores."

"Thank you." She stood up and shook out the shirt. "Are you ready for lunch?"

"No, I ate at the Ortegas'. I hope I didn't wake you when I left."

"I didn't hear a thing until the alarm went off at six." She hung the shirt on a hanger.

Travis came closer. "What are you doing with my shirt?"

"There was a tear. I repaired it."

"Let me see. Hey, a crown." He held the shirt in front of him. "Just like the Monarch Ranch brand. Look where it falls—right over my heart. That was clever of you."

Cindy felt her chest swell with pride. Get a grip, she told herself. So Travis could be charming, after all. So what? One little compliment would not be enough to make her fall at his feet. "Thank you," she said, loading her voice with even more frost.

"You're welcome." He eyed the dresses and aprons hanging on the rack by the laundry door. "You've been busy."

"Yes." He didn't have to look so surprised. She'd always given a day's work for a day's pay, no matter what first impression he'd gotten. She took the shirt from him and hung it with the other clothes. "Do you eat breakfast so early every day? You don't have to go to the bunkhouse. I don't mind getting up at five and cooking breakfast for you here."

"Thanks, but that won't be necessary. I'm not usually such an early bird. I just had trouble getting to sleep last night—strange bed, I guess. I haven't been at the ranch in months." He walked to the counter and leaned against it. Crossing his arms over his chest, he leveled his gaze at her. "Cindy. Miss Ellerbee. There's something we need to talk about."

Those blue eyes were hypnotic when focused so intently, Cindy noticed. "Is there?" she asked.

"Yes. Why don't you sit down?"

"All right." She pulled out one of the kitchen chairs and sat. "What do you want to talk about?"

"Your job."

She'd been expecting it. Still, it came as a shock. "You're going to ask for my resignation."

Travis shot her a puzzled look. "Resignation? What gave you that idea?"

"You have every right. I slept in your bed. I yelled at you. I hit you with a spoon—although you deserved that. But please don't think I'm typical of At Your Service employees. I'm sure if you called today, Fae Rae could have a replacement here by the end of the week."

"You can't go! I don't want a replacement. I want you—" he cleared his throat "—to stay. Here. You're doing a fine job."

"I am?" Relief flowed through her. She did not want to leave the ranch, not yet. She needed a little more time before she'd be ready to make her way in the world on her terms.

"You are." He paused, frowning. "Except for one thing."

"What thing?"

"Gus tells me you can't drive a standard shift car."

"No. I can't."

"There are three vehicles in the garage. Two of them have standard shifts. They all need to be driven."

"They do?"

"Yes."

"Why?"

"To keep the batteries charged and the engines oiled. Things like that."

"Couldn't one of the ranch hands do that?"

"They could, but it would take time away from their regular chores. Don't you want to learn how to drive the pickup truck and the Bronco?"

"Well, yes. But who would teach me? One of the cowboys? Won't that take time from their work, too?"

"Not if I do it."

Cindy wiped her suddenly damp palms on her apron. "Oh, no. I couldn't ask you—"

He held up a hand. "Stop. You don't have to ask. I'm volunteering. Teaching you to drive will give me something useful to do until Mom and the others arrive."

"Well, if you're sure this is a good idea...."

"I am. We can start right now." He looked her over. "As soon as you change."

Cindy looked down at her serviceable gray dress and her starched white apron. "What's wrong with this?"

"The skirt's too full. I won't be able to see your

legs—I mean your feet. Have to be able to see your feet on the accelerator and the clutch.''

''Oh. So I should wear pants?''

''Shorts would work, too.''

She untied her apron and hung it on the pantry door. ''I'll be right back. There's fresh coffee, and I made a pecan coffee cake.''

Cindy walked to her room and stripped off her dress. She went to the closet and pulled a pair of lightweight white cotton trousers and a pale yellow T-shirt off their hangers.

Within minutes she was back in the kitchen. Travis was seated at the table, munching on a piece of coffee cake. When he saw her, he brushed the crumbs from his fingers and stood up. ''Ready?''

''As I'll ever be.''

''No need to be nervous. After all, there's no traffic way out here.''

''It's not traffic that's making me nervous,'' she muttered, following him out the door and into the garage. The thought of spending time with Travis, in the close confines of a car—that was making her jumpy. ''Which one?'' she asked, stopping behind the Bronco.

''The truck.''

''Okay.'' She started for the passenger side of the black pickup.

''Not that way. You drive.''

Her brows shot upward. ''Backward?''

''Maybe you're right. I'll back out of the garage, then you can take over.'' He got into the cab, leaving Cindy standing in the garage.

She followed him outside. ''You know what? I don't think it's necessary for you to waste time teaching me how to drive. All I really need to know is how to start the various vehicles, right? How hard can that be? I can do the Cadillac now. Just show me how to start the other two, and I'll be all set. The engines will oil themselves, and the batteries will—"

Travis got out of the truck and stood in front of her, holding the truck door open. "Too dangerous. You can't sit in a car with its engine running in a garage. Haven't you ever heard of carbon monoxide poisoning?" He shifted his gaze to a spot over her left shoulder. "Besides, the wheels have to turn if you want the oil to circulate and the electrical system to get a workout."

"Oh. I didn't realize…"

"That's okay. No one expected you to be a mechanic. And I don't look at this as a waste of time. This is necessary to preserve and protect valuable equipment."

"Well, when you put it that way." Cindy gave up and climbed into the driver's seat. When he'd climbed into the passenger seat, she asked, "What do I do now?"

"See those three pedals? You know about two of them, the brake and the accelerator. The one on the left is the clutch." He scooted next to her, putting his arm on the back of the driver's seat. Taking her hand, he placed it on the gear shift, keeping his hand on top of hers. "See the diagram on the knob, here?"

Cindy nodded. She couldn't speak. Her throat was so dry nothing but a croak would come out if she tried. How could she concentrate on the lesson when his hip was touching hers, his arm was around her shoulders and his hand was on top of hers? She squeezed her eyes shut and thought about the first time Etienne had touched her.

She'd gotten weak in the knees that time, too. And look what that weakness had cost her—her job, her reputation. She could not, would not, let that happen again.

"Cindy? Are you listening?"

Cindy opened her eyes and stiffened her spine. Never again, she repeated. Once had been one time too many. She couldn't even blame Travis for her inappropriate reaction to his touch. He hadn't done anything out of line. This was a driving lesson, not an attempted seduction, for heaven's sake. "Yes, of course. First gear, second, third and reverse. I heard every word you said. What next?"

"Start her up, and I'll show you."

A few miles down the road, Cindy had built up an immunity to his touch, his voice and his teaching methods. She had had more than enough of Travis Rule and his driving lesson. "Have you ever taught anyone anything?" Cindy yelled.

"I've taught lots of people lots of things," Travis yelled back.

"I don't believe you! You're mean and rude and you don't give clear instructions."

"You don't listen! How many times do I have to tell you—" He grabbed the wheel. "Look out! You almost ran us off the road."

"How do I stop this thing?" Cindy was so angry, she was close to tears. But no way would she let this crazy man see her cry!

"Step on the clutch—"

Cindy ignored him. She hated the clutch. The middle doohicky was the brake. She slammed her foot down hard on that pedal. The truck shuddered to a stop.

"—then the brake."

"Is it off?"

"Yeah. You killed it. Again." Travis turned his head and stared out the passenger-side window.

Where did he get off acting disgusted? None of this fiasco was her fault. She hadn't done anything wrong. She *never* did anything wrong! She'd always been a good student. But she'd always had good teachers up to now.

Travis Rule was not a good teacher.

How had the man ever gotten to be The Richest Bachelor in Texas? He couldn't do anything right, and, judging by the way he'd been treating her for the past half hour, he must blame his subordinates for his failures.

Well, he could take his driving lessons and go to blazes! Cindy opened the door and got out. Slamming the door shut, she started walking back toward the ranch.

"Where do you think you're going?" Travis shouted.

"Home." She heard the truck start up. Moving to the side of the dirt road, she kept walking.

Seconds later the pickup pulled alongside her.

Leaning out the window, Travis said, "You can't walk home. We're miles from the ranch house. Come on, Cindy, get back in the truck, and I'll take you back. We'll give it another try tomorrow."

"No." To put some distance between them, she walked off the roadway into the ditch. "Go away."

"I'm not leaving you out here by yourself. You could get heat stroke."

"I'm cool as a cucumber." She was sweating like a pig.

"You could get bitten by a snake."

"I'll bite first." Cindy couldn't stop a nervous look at her feet. She'd see a snake before she stepped on it, wouldn't she?

"Aw, Cindy, give it up—"

Cindy whirled around, intending to give Travis a piece of her mind. She whirled a little too fast. She tripped over her own feet and sat down. Hard.

In a cactus. A prickly pear cactus.

# 4

---

Travis was out of the truck and standing over her almost before she realized where she'd landed. "Ouch. Ow. *Ouch!* Ohmigod, ohmigod." Cindy struggled to get up and out of the reach of the hundreds of tiny thorns working themselves into her bottom, her thighs, her hands. Every inch of her backside smarted, stung, *hurt.*

Travis grabbed her by the elbows and pulled her up. "Cindy, sweetheart. Are you all right?"

"No. I am not all right. I am in excruciating pain. I fell in a cactus. Ow! It hurts!"

"I know it does. Come on, let's get you back to the ranch. We'll call the doctor." He ushered her toward the truck and opened the passenger door. "Get in."

Cindy stared at the seat. "How? I can't sit down." She backed away from the truck. "I'll walk."

"You will not walk! I'll help you up, and you won't have to sit." Travis grabbed her around the waist and hoisted her into the pickup.

Cindy ended up kneeling on the bench seat, facing the rear window. "I can't hold on, either. My hands are full of thorns. How can there be so many? And why are they so small?'' She stared at her palms. ''I can feel them, but I can barely see most of them.''

Travis climbed into the driver's seat. Pointing to one of the many pear cacti on the side of the road, he said, ''Look at the cacti. See those tufts around the edges? Those are the ones that are hard to see, not the big ones on the flat surfaces. Lean forward against the seat.''

She followed his instructions, gripping the back of the seat with her elbows. ''G-Gus told me about b-burning pear cactuses during droughts so that the cattle could eat them. Now I understand. Think of a poor c-cow getting a mouthful of these—it would be like eating needles. Stinging needles. Ow! Ow! Ow!''

''Take it easy, Cindy. I'll take care of you, as soon as we get home. I know what to do. Same thing happened to Treat once.''

''You pushed him into a cactus, too?''

''A horse threw him and he landed on one. I didn't push you.''

''Yes, you did. Oh, I know you didn't touch me, but you pushed me. Verbally.''

''All I said was—never mind. I'm sorry. Guess I'm not very good at driver's education.''

''You're a terrible teacher,'' she agreed. She hadn't been a very good student, either, but she'd never tell him that. She'd have to admit that his blue eyes and sexy mouth had blown her concentration to pieces.

To her dismay, she'd found that being in close proximity to Travis Rule stirred feelings she hadn't felt since the first time Etienne had charmed her. Every time that unruly lock of brown hair had fallen across his forehead, her fingers had fairly itched to smooth it back in place. But Travis had definitely not been trying to charm her.

He'd been rude, overbearing and loud, shouting unintelligible instructions at her.

All in all, he'd shown more consideration for the truck than for her.

And she'd been charmed in spite of herself. That had her trembling in her tennis shoes, scared that history might repeat itself. She'd only just recovered from her last encounter with a charmer. She would not go through that again, not after she'd spent weeks making plans for a brand-new life, one that did not require a man. What kind of fool would forget both her past and her future for some brief, meaningless liaison in the present?

Not her. She was smarter than that. Strong, too. She could take care of herself, all by herself.

Except now, when every inch of her body stung and itched and hurt. "How much longer?"

"We'll be there soon. Hold on, Cindy. I don't want to drive too fast, not with you having to make the trip on your knees. I'm sorry the driving lesson turned into such a disaster."

"I forgive you," she said magnanimously. "I suppose I should apologize, too. I shouldn't have yelled at you."

"I didn't mind. No one yells at me anymore. I kind of liked it. Brought back good memories. Mom used to holler her head off at me. And Dad. And Treat. We always knew exactly what she expected of us. Not any longer. Now she's quiet and refined. But still stubborn as ever. You're a lot like her in that respect."

Cindy ignored that statement. He could call her

stubborn all he wanted to. As far as she was concerned, being stubborn was a virtue, one that would keep her on a straight path to her goal.

Travis continued to drive slowly, so Cindy could keep her balance, but he got them back to the ranch house within minutes. He helped her out of the pickup and into the house. "I'm pretty sure I know how to handle this, but I'll call Doc Frazier and check. Hold on just a minute, honey."

Cindy waited, not patiently, while he dialed the number. The burning, stinging sensation made it hard to stand still. She paced up and down the hall while he talked to the doctor.

"Doc. It's Travis Rule." There was a pause, then Travis continued, "Yeah, I'm here for a week or two. Listen, we've got a little problem here...."

Cindy stopped listening and concentrated on holding her fingers apart. The tiny thorns between her fingers hurt the most, for some reason. Travis hung up the telephone.

"What did he say?" asked Cindy, grimacing.

"That we should get those thorns out of you."

"For that he went to medical school? I could have told you that. Did he say how?"

"Same way we got them out of Treat. First, take off your clothes."

She backed up. "I beg your pardon?"

"Some of the thorns will be dislodged that way. Next, take a shower. That will get rid of more of them. The rest..."

"Yes?"

"Dr. Frazier suggested tweezers and a magnifying glass. Most of the thorns are tiny like little hairs, hard to see."

"Tweezers! Did the doctor suggest how I am supposed to reach around—"

Travis stopped her with a sheepish grin.

Cindy gasped. "Oh, no! You're not going to pluck thorns from my bare bottom."

"Be reasonable, Cindy. You can't do it. There's no one else around."

"Dolores—"

"—is visiting her sister in Eagle Pass. She and the kids left right after lunch. She won't be back until late tonight. You could ask Gus, but I don't think he'd do it. He'd be too embarrassed."

"He's not the only one," Cindy muttered. "Why can't you drive me into town? The doctor can get rid of the thorns."

"Do you really want to spend an hour on your knees in the car?"

"N-no, I guess not."

"Look, I know I've been out of line with you a time or two. But this is a medical emergency. I swear I won't take advantage of the situation. Think of me as a doctor. We'll drape you with a sheet, and I'll only look at the patch of skin I'm working on. I'm pretty sure there's a magnifying glass in the desk in the library." He ducked into the room and returned in a flash holding a magnifying glass. "Got it. Ready when you are, Miss Ellerbee."

"Oh, all right." What choice did she have? None. Travis sounded stern and not a little put out. No wonder—she was behaving like a nervous spinster. Hadn't she decided once and for all to be an independent single woman, able to take care of herself?

Yes. But she hadn't factored cactus thorns in her backside into her plan. Right this minute she needed help. And Travis was the only game in town. Resigned, Cindy led the way to her room. She held out her hands. "Start with these. I can't get undressed until I can use my hands. They itch like crazy."

"Do you have tweezers?"

"Yes, in the top cabinet drawer in the bathroom."

"I'll be right back."

Cindy had never wanted to sit down more than she did at that moment. She looked longingly at the chair in the corner of her bedroom. Her hands, her buttocks and the backs of her thighs alternately stung and itched. She'd never been so miserable in her life. She couldn't even brush away the tears trickling down her face, not without risking transferring some of the tiny cactus thorns to her face or her eyes. She blinked rapidly, trying to halt the flow.

She did not want Travis to see a strong, independent woman like her crying like a baby.

"Here we go. Aw, Cindy, don't cry."

"I'm not c-crying."

"I know you're not. Where's a tissue?"

"There." She pointed to the dresser.

Travis pulled one from the box and dabbed at Cindy's cheeks. "Good thing you kept your hands away from your face."

"Please get the thorns out. I can't take much more of this." She bit her lip. First crying. Now whining. Lucky for her she wasn't trying to impress Travis with stoic fortitude.

"Give me your hand."

She held out her right hand, fingers spread apart. Most of the thorns were in her palm, but the most painful ones were lodged between her fingers. Holding the magnifying glass over her palm, Travis began plucking the hairlike thorns. "I'm not hurting you, am I?"

"N-no."

"I think that's all for that hand." He reached for her other hand.

Cindy flexed her fingers, cramping from being held apart for so long.

"Better?"

"Yes. Thank you."

A few minutes later, Travis declared her hands thorn free. "Okay, Cindy. Time for that shower. I'll get a sheet from the linen closet and bring it to you."

Cindy retreated to the bathroom and took off the thin cotton pants. She should have worn jeans. Thorns probably couldn't penetrate denim. Next time she'd know better than to wear gauzy cotton pants.

What was she thinking? There wasn't going to be a next time. She never would fall into a cactus again—hopefully that was a once-in-a-lifetime occurrence.

Stripping off the rest of her clothes, she tried looking over her shoulder into the mirror to see if she could remove any of the thorns herself. She managed to reach a few of the larger ones, the only ones she'd ever noticed on the cactus before today. Who would have guessed that those soft-looking tufts sprouting on the edges of the cactus pad could be so painful?

And so invisible. She could feel the little suckers, but she couldn't see them. With a resigned sigh, Cindy gave up on self-help. She turned on the water and stepped into the shower. The tepid stream cooled the stinging sensation, persuading her to stay in the shower until she heard a knock on the bathroom door.

"Cindy? I've got a sheet for you."

"Just a minute." Turning off the water, she stepped out of the tub and reached for a towel. She held it in front of her as she opened the door a crack. "Let me have it." That came out like a strangled groan. Clearing her throat, she added, "Please."

Travis pushed the sheet through the small opening and she shut the door.

Drying herself, at least her front and the backs of her shoulders, she wrapped the sheet around her loosely, with the opening in the rear. The temporary relief provided by the shower had ceased the minute she stepped out of the tub. Now the stinging and the itching were back with a vengeance.

As much as she wanted to cower in the bathroom for several more hours, she couldn't do it. She had to let Travis get rid of the thorns.

Cindy opened the door and peered into the bedroom. Travis was standing with his back to her, next to the bed. "Umm. I'm ready. I guess."

He turned around. "Good. Come over here and lie down on your stomach."

"Lie down? On the bed? Can't I stand up?"

"If you're standing, I'll have to kneel. This could take a while. I don't think my knees could tolerate it. You might get tired of standing, too."

"You're probably right." She stepped around him and climbed onto the bed, awkwardly because she had one hand behind her back holding the edges of the sheet together. Finally she managed to lie down on the bed. Burying her face in the pillow she said, "Okay. I'm ready. Do it."

She felt the mattress sag as Travis sat on the edge of the bed.

"Let go of the sheet, Cindy."

She gripped the sheet tighter. "I can't."

He reached for her hand and pried her fingers loose. "I'm going to start with your thighs and work my way up."

Cindy felt him arrange the sheet so that her legs were exposed to his view. She could feel her face get warm. No need to get embarrassed, she told herself. He'd seen her legs before. She flinched when the tweezers touched her thigh. "Sorry. Did I hurt you?"

"No, the tweezers are cold. That's why I jumped." Not because his fingers brushed her thigh. Hadn't she reminded herself only an hour or two ago that she did not need or want a man in her life? She had. Therefore, the touch of a man like Travis Rule would not make her skittish. The tweezers had made her jump.

"I should have realized—doctors warm their instruments, don't they?"

"Not all of them."

"Maybe if I held them under hot water for a minute or two—"

"That's not necessary. The tweezers aren't icy cold."

"I should have sterilized them. I will sterilize them."

She felt the bed jiggle again as Travis got up. If she didn't know better, she'd think he was as nervous as she was about this. "Travis, stop frittering around. Just do it."

"You're sure?"

"Positive. I hurt. I want to stop hurting."

He sat down next to her. "Oh, lordy. Here's something else I'm not very good at—doctoring."

Cindy managed to keep from jumping the next time she felt the tweezers. "You must be good at something. You are The Richest Bachelor in Texas. You didn't inherit your wealth.''

"Yes, I did. Some of it. Most of it I made on my own. A lot of it's on paper, you know.''

"What's on paper?''

"My supposed wealth.''

"You're not really rich?''

"I don't have billions, not the kind you can spend, anyway.''

"What other kind is there?''

"Stock, stock options. Future earnings. Appreciated assets. That kind of wealth.''

"But you're not poor.''

He chuckled. "No, Cindy, I'm not poor. I could support a wife, maybe even a kid or two. Interested?''

"No. I don't intend to marry. Not ever.''

"Why not? Did some guy break your heart?''

"None of your business.''

"I suppose not. No one ever broke my heart, and I never thought I wanted to get married, either. But lately I've been having second thoughts.''

Cindy bit her lip to keep from asking what kind of second thoughts. She didn't care about Travis's marriage plans. Not at all. Nothing to do with her whether The Richest Bachelor in Texas gave up his title for a wedding band.

Travis continued gently tweezing the thorns from the backs of her legs. "What would make you have second thoughts, Cindy? Falling in love?''

Cindy raised her head off the pillow and shook it violently. "Been there. Done that. Don't want to do it again. I'm not even sure I believe in love.''

"I believe. I've seen it. You will, too, if Mom and Dad ever spend time here with you. However, after an extensive study of the subject, I've decided love only happens to the lucky few.''

Cindy laid her head down again and closed her eyes. ''That makes sense. I think my parents loved each other, too. I remember they kissed a lot.'' She sighed wistfully. ''I'm not one of the lucky ones.''

''Neither am I. But there are other reasons to get married. Companionship. Children. If you were going to look for a husband, how would you go about it?''

''I wouldn't. I told you. I'm never getting married.''

''You don't want a family of your own?''

''No. That's a cliché.''

''What?''

''That all orphans long to be part of a family. I don't.'' Not anymore. Not since she'd learned that families closed ranks against outsiders.

''Humor me. Pretend that you do. I am the one wielding the tweezers, remember. Hypothetically speaking, how would you recognize the right man for you? Your man, so to speak?''

''I wouldn't ask to see his bank book,'' Cindy said with a sniff.

''You've made that clear. Would you see stars, do you think? Hear bells? Singing, maybe?''

''Of course not. Bells, stars—things like that happen in fairy tales, not in real life.''

''How would you find the right man, then?'' he persisted.

''This is a silly conversation. I'm not looking for a man to marry, but if I were, I'm sure I'd know him.''

''Right away? Or would it take a while?''

"I think it would take a while. First impressions aren't always right. Are you almost finished?"

"Almost. My mother has come up with several unique ideas for me to find my mate. Treat's favorite was the contest. Mom suggested that I sponsor an essay competition—why I want to marry Travis Rule in twenty-five words or less—and choose the lucky winner."

"You're not serious?"

"Mom was. We talked her out of it. Then Treat said I could come up with better tests, tests that would demonstrate a woman's ability to perform wifely duties. He mentioned cooking and sex as the primary ones. Treat thought I should give the final in the bedroom."

"That's disgusting!"

"That's what I said. But I haven't completely given up on the testing idea."

"Well, you should. In the first place, what kind of woman would agree to be tested? She'd have to be a fool."

"Hmm. Good point."

"In the second place, what kind of tests are there for honor, responsibility, desire…warmth?"

"Aha! You do know what kind of man would ring your bell! You want a man who's honest, dependable and sexy."

"I beg your pardon. I do not want any man. And I didn't say one word about sex."

"Sex, desirability. Same thing."

"Even if I could come up with tests, I don't believe any man alive could pass them all."

"Present company excepted, of course. I have all those qualities you named."

"I'm sure you do. And a few others, like arrogant, conceited and spoiled."

"Ouch. I'll shut up now." After what seemed like hours, he said, "I think that's all for your legs. Do you feel any I missed?"

"I don't know. Every inch of my backside either stings or itches."

"It's time to move on."

"Yes. What are you waiting for?"

"Remember, Cindy, this is necessary. It's not like I'm going to enjoy seeing your naked bu—derriere."

He sounded...anxious. Cindy squeezed her eyes shut. She could take it. And she would not let him embarrass her, either. "Go ahead, Travis. Knock yourself out."

"Cindy, look at me."

Twisting her head around, she looked.

He waved the tweezers under her nose. "I am not having fun, Miss Ellerbee. Trust me. Having you naked on a bed and not being able to do anything with you except this—" he plucked out a thorn "—is not my idea of a good time."

Cindy turned her face away from him. Her cheeks burned. Why hadn't she kept her mouth shut? Now that her nudity had been exposed, so to speak, her body shimmered with sexual tension. She could feel it in every inch of her bare skin.

Travis continued plucking thorns in silence. "I'm sorry. I didn't mean to embarrass you."

"I'm not embarrassed." Her words were muffled by the pillow.

"You're blushing," he said.

She raised her head and peeked over her shoulder. "How can you tell? I had my face hidden."

"That's not the only place you blush, honey," he said gently. Clearing his throat, he added, "Let's talk about something else."

"Good idea." She winced as he touched the tweezers to her bottom one more time. "And don't call me honey. That's the second or third time you've done that, and I don't like it. You're a doctor, remember? Medical emergency?"

"Yeah. Talk to me, Cindy. Conversation will keep my mind from thinking nondoctorlike thoughts."

"What do you want to talk about? You?"

"Not especially. I know about me. Let's talk about…your bookcase. Why do you have all the how-to books on business?"

"I don't plan to be a housekeeper all my life."

"You want a corporate job instead? I could probably find you—"

"No, thanks. I want to be my own boss."

"Ah! An entrepreneur. What kind of business? A maid service?"

"No. A needlework shop."

"Dolores said you were very handy with a needle. And I saw what you did with my shirt. So tell me about your shop, Cindy. Do you have a business plan?"

"I plan to open a shop and sell needlework supplies. I'll also give lessons, and I'll sell the things I make myself. What kind of business plan?"

"Projections of expenses and earnings for the first couple of years. Where to get the best terms for a line of credit. You're not planning on opening a shop in Carrizo or Crystal, are you?"

"No, I thought a larger city. Houston, or San Antonio. Dallas, maybe."

"Have you compared the cost of leasing space in those cities? Labor costs? You'll need at least one clerk to handle sales while you're teaching classes. How about space? How much will you need? Would your customer base be more likely to shop at a mall or in a stand-alone storefront?"

"Stop! I don't know. Your questions are making me feel insecure and unprepared."

"Sorry. I didn't mean to do that. I was trying to help." He plucked a few more thorns. "Tell you what. I'll have my marketing people check into a few things for you. And I'll show you how to work up a business plan."

Cindy raised her head off the pillow and looked at him. "I couldn't ask you to do that, share your time and experience with me."

"You don't have to ask. I'm volunteering. If it would make you feel better, I'll think up something for you to do for me." He must have felt her muscles tense. "Don't worry. Nothing illegal or immoral. Is it a deal?"

"I guess so. Yes. Of course. It's very nice of you to offer."

"Glad to be of service. I think I've gotten all the thorns. Feel any I've missed?"

"No. But it's hard to tell. I still itch. Everywhere."

"I'll take care of that. Don't move."

The bed jiggled as he got up. Cindy heard the bathroom door open and close. Then he sat on the bed again, this time closer, so that his thigh touched hers.

"Ooooh! What are you doing?"

"Rubbing calamine lotion on. Feels good, doesn't it?"

The stinging and itching were fading away. Cindy

couldn't be sure whether her relief was due to the calamine lotion or Travis's touch. His hands moving on her buttocks and her thighs were making her pulse race and her breathing shallow. "Good," she agreed, reluctantly.

"Roll over on your back. See if you feel any thorns I missed."

She rolled onto her back, tangling her arms in the sheet as she did so. Travis was leaning over her, so close she could see the gold flecks in his blue eyes.

"Feel anything?" he asked.

"Oh, yes," she sighed. She felt as if she might shatter into a million pieces, each piece throbbing with something she'd never felt before...not desire—need. She *needed* Travis Rule's hands on her body. And that wasn't all. She needed his mouth on hers.

"Where? What did I miss?"

Shocked by her wanton thoughts, Cindy couldn't speak. She could feel her face growing warm. She wanted to pull the sheet over her head, but she couldn't move her arms. All she could do was stare wide-eyed at Travis.

Whatever he saw there made his blue eyes darken. "Cindy." He groaned her name. "I have to do this—"

That tempting mouth was on hers. And her lips promptly yielded to temptation, molding themselves compliantly to his. Her arms magically freed themselves from the tangled sheets, wrapping themselves around his neck and pulling him on top of her. Her heart pounded, sending her blood racing even faster through her veins. She forgot she had little use for men, none at all for this man. She forgot how to breathe. Her whole body was betraying her.

Treason felt good.

So did Travis. His chest rested on her breasts, and his legs tangled with hers, crushing her into the bed. He deepened the kiss, his tongue plunging into her mouth. Travis filled her senses with his taste, his touch, his smell.

His hand found her breast, cupped it, coaxing the nipple into a hard bud. She arched against him. She had to get closer to that touch.

No!

Cindy shoved him off the bed.

She leaned over the edge of the bed, clutching the sheet to her heaving chest. "Get out! You were going to treat me like a doctor. You promised! Some doctor you are! What oath did you take? Not the Hippocratic—the Hypocrite, more likely. Get up off the floor and leave this room, you...you *man!*"

## 5

Travis lay flat on his back, dazed.

He was in deep trouble.

This time the choir had been accompanied by a full symphony orchestra. He stared up at Cindy. Her lips were pink and swollen from his kisses, but her gray eyes were stormy.

Leaning over the edge of the bed, she looked at him like he was something she'd found under a rock. "I want you to leave. And don't you ever kiss me again!"

Apparently, Cindy had not heard the music.

But it hadn't all been one-sided. "You kissed me back," he pointed out mildly.

"Are you going to leave?"

He stayed on the floor. "Not just yet. Why did you kiss me, Cindy?"

She flopped onto her back, out of his line of vision. "I don't know. I'm weak. First, Etienne. Now you. I thought I'd gotten stronger these past few months. I really did. But—"

"Who is Etienne?" Travis sat up. He wanted to see her face when she told him.

"Please, Travis. I want you to go." Her chin trembled.

"Don't cry, Cindy." He wanted to take her in his arms again. To comfort her, not to ravish her.

Like she'd believe that.

She'd scream the house down if he touched her again.

"I'm not crying? Why would I cry? Over you? Ha!" She crossed her arms over her chest and stared at the ceiling.

"Your chin was quivering."

"Because I'm angry, not because I'm about to bawl."

"You're mad at me."

"Yes." After a brief pause, she added, "And myself. Mostly myself."

She didn't sound quite so angry. He stood up. "I'll leave you alone for now, but don't even think about leaving here." He cleared his throat. That sounded suspiciously like an order, even to him. "I mean, promise me you'll stay."

She closed her eyes. He thought she might be counting to ten. "All right. I promise. But no more kisses."

"Mmm." She could take that noncommittal noise any way she wanted, but *he* wasn't making any promises. Travis stood up and walked out of her bedroom, closing the door behind him.

That was as far as he got before it hit him.

He *had* fallen in love at first sight.

The spectacular kiss he'd shared with *his woman* had confirmed what the angelic choir had tried to tell him...when? Only yesterday? Couldn't be. He'd known Cindy forever. He had always loved her.

That was why none of those other women had stood a snowball's chance in hell with him.

But Cindy didn't love him.

And she hadn't answered his question. Who was Etienne?

He ruthlessly suppressed the sick, jealous feeling generated by the mere thought of Cindy with another man. He'd worry about that later. For now, he had more important things to consider.

What next?

Did he tell her about the choir? Confess he loved her? That made him feel sick in a different way. Woozy. Almost as if he were...scared. Not that he was. A grown man, a man of foresight and wisdom, a successful businessman, would never be afraid of a mere woman.

Who was he kidding? Cindy and the emotions she inspired terrified him.

He could not risk telling her how he felt. Not yet. Not until he had some inkling she felt the same way. But she *had* kissed him back. That was real, not his overactive imagination at work. She'd stopped kissing him when—what? When he'd pounced on her like a starving man at a banquet. Some great lover he was, taking advantage of a woman weakened by pain. No wonder she'd kicked him out of bed.

Cindy had accused him of being like Etienne. Had some other creep taken advantage of her? What was he to Cindy? And while he was asking dumb questions, what kind of moniker was that for a real man? *Etienne.* Sounded like a sissy name to him. On the other hand, Cindy had lived in New Orleans. Etienne must be French. Had his woman fallen for a suave, sophisticated seducer?

Travis put his ear to Cindy's bedroom door. What was she doing? Crying? Packing? He couldn't hear anything. Slowly he opened the door, prepared to duck in case she threw something at him. He peeked through the crack.

She was on her stomach, the sheet twisted around her. Cindy appeared to be asleep. He pushed the door open wider, and the hinges creaked. She didn't stir.

Poor baby must be exhausted from her run-in with the cactus and with him.

Travis slipped quietly into the room and pulled the blanket over her. Sighing deeply, he sat down in the chair in the corner of the room and watched her sleep.

Lovesick.

That's what he was. Pitiful and lovesick. And he didn't have any idea what to do about it.

How did a man go about making a woman fall in love with him? Was it even possible to *make* love happen? Based on his past experience, he would not have thought so. Plenty of women had tried their best to trip him into falling in love.

Travis got up and left Cindy's room. He had to think clearly, and seeing her sprawled bonelessly on the bed, her silky dark hair fanned on the pillow, was too distracting. He went to his office and paced.

He had to believe Cindy felt something for him. Before she'd kicked him out of bed, she had kissed him. With some enthusiasm, he remembered. He'd begin with that and build on it. And he had another advantage—she'd told him what she wanted in a mate. A man who was honest, dependable and desirable.

His mistake had been in starting from the wrong end of her list. Instead of trying to make her want him as much as he wanted her, he should have told her about being an Eagle Scout. But he'd moved too fast, too soon, and he sure hadn't acted like a Boy Scout. No wonder she'd panicked.

He had to look at things from her point of view. Since no one was singing in her ear, she had no reason to know he was her soul mate. Face it, she had to be thinking of him as a stranger.

Except she had read his baby book.

Travis stopped pacing in front of the library table. There they were, two blue albums, one for him and one for Treat. At least she knew he'd been a cute baby.

He picked up one of the scrapbooks and flipped through it. Sure enough, it was filled with his exploits. Eagle Scout, quarterback of the champion football team, valedictorian. And that was only high school. If she'd read the baby books, Cindy must have looked at all the photo albums and scrapbooks. She had to know the kind of man he was.

Yeah. She did. Cindy had called him arrogant, conceited and spoiled. He'd assumed she was teasing.

Maybe not.

So he had a few faults. But he had virtues, too, every single one she'd listed. She wanted honest. He was honest. And dependable. And sexy. He shoved his hand through his hair and groaned.

And maybe a little conceited. Hell, nobody was perfect.

He had other qualities she might come to appreciate. He could take care of her, and not only financially. Emotionally, physically, every way a man could take care of a woman. And she'd get more than him. He had a great family, one that would welcome her with open arms.

Travis frowned. Except for Treat. Treat could damn

well keep his arms at his sides when he was around Cindy.

Okay, so he had a few things going for him. How would Cindy find out about his good qualities? He thought for a few minutes. What did he have that she wanted?

Not his body. Yet.

But she might be interested in his mind. Add *smart* to the list, he told himself with a grin. Cindy wanted her own business. He had his own business. He could teach her things she needed to know to make her needlework shop a success.

Whistling, Travis headed for the kitchen.

Cindy woke with a start. She sat up, remembering everything.

Travis! He'd kissed her. More than once, and not only on the lips. And she'd let him. Let him? She'd encouraged him. Blatantly, wantonly.

She was a wicked woman.

And a reckless one. What on earth had she been thinking? That she'd find happiness and fulfillment in the arms of the man she'd pegged as arrogant, spoiled and patronizing? A man who said he never wanted to marry one minute, then talked about giving tests to prospective brides the next?

There was something very wrong with her. Her first romance had ended in disaster because she'd trusted too easily. When Etienne had betrayed her, she'd thought her broken heart would never heal. It had, faster than she would have expected. But here she was, ready to fracture it all over again.

Good night, Nellie!

She was not only too dumb to learn from her past mistakes, she was also fickle.

A knock sounded on the door. "Cindy? Are you awake?"

Clutching the sheet to her breast, she called out, "Yes."

The door opened a crack. "Dinner's almost ready. Do you want me to bring you a tray?"

"Dinner?" She looked at the clock on her bedside table. It read six-thirty. She'd slept for hours. "No, thank you. I'll be out in a minute."

"Okay. How do you feel?"

"Groggy." And stupid. She ought to write to the Hufstatler sisters and tell them to include a course on male behavior in the curriculum. Surely she wouldn't be in this position, again, if she'd had a normal adolescence. But the girls at the orphans' home had not been allowed to date.

Some of them, including her, might have broken the rule, if the opportunity had ever presented itself. Unfortunately, there hadn't been many boys around. Most of her classmates had gone on to college, or to jobs which put them in contact with boys their own ages. She'd stayed another two years to attend the Nanny School. No men there, either. And once she'd begun working for the Frerets, she hadn't had time for a social life of her own. She'd only had Sundays and Thursday evenings off.

No wonder she'd fallen for Etienne. He was the first man who'd ever paid any attention to her.

But his kisses hadn't affected her like Travis's had. Cindy bit back a moan. She got hot all over again just thinking about the things his tempting mouth had done to her. She looked in the mirror. Travis was right. She did blush other places besides her face.

Her stomach grumbled, reminding her that it was past dinnertime. Travis had cooked dinner? And he'd been ready to serve it to her on a tray? Cindy felt her insides go mushy.

She tightened her abdominals. "Don't give him too much credit—after dinner in bed, he'd probably expect me to be his dessert."

She got up and went to the bathroom. Splashing cold water on her face, she thought about climbing out the window and walking to the bunkhouse. Gus would take her to town. She could get a bus for San Antonio, then catch a flight to New Orleans—

She'd promised him she wouldn't leave.

Surely a promise made in the aftermath of passion didn't count? She could not stay here. Alone with him. She'd never be able to resist him again. She wasn't sure even now how she'd come up with the strength to push him away. If he hadn't touched her...there. Luckily, he had. The touch of his hand on her breast had been what shocked her out of her sensual fog.

She didn't have to stay. She'd call Fae Rae and ask her to send a replacement, right away. Travis could survive for a few days on his own. He knew how to take care of himself. He even knew how to cook. Yeah, right. He'd probably broiled a steak and baked a potato. Big deal. Any fool could do that.

Cindy squared her shoulders. She would get dressed, go to the kitchen and sit across the table from him. She would eat the meal he'd prepared because she needed to keep her strength up, and she was feeling a little weak.

Then she'd tell him she quit.

"You're up," said Travis as she walked into the kitchen. "How do you feel?"

"Fine. Better. Okay." Travis held out a chair for her, and she sat down.

"I'll get the food on the table right away. You must be starved."

"I could eat," she grudgingly admitted.

Travis retrieved a bowl of salad from the refrigerator and set it on the table. "Help yourself." He went to the stove.

Filling her bowl with salad, Cindy watched him take a casserole dish out of the oven. A spicy aroma reached her nostrils. "What are we having?"

"Enchiladas." He put the bubbling casserole on the table, adding, "I'll just get the tortillas out of the microwave, and we're all set. Would you like a beer, or iced tea?"

"Tea, please." She had to keep a clear head. Travis really did know how to cook. She took a bite of her enchilada, to make sure. Delicious. "Delicious," she repeated aloud as Travis sat down opposite her. "Who taught you to cook?"

"Mom. And Gus."

"They did a good job."

Serving himself a huge helping of enchiladas, Travis asked casually, "Who is Etienne?"

Cindy choked on a bite of tortilla. "What?"

"Etienne. Who is he?"

"A man I knew in New Orleans. Etienne Breaux. Mercedes Freret's brother."

"And Mercedes Freret would be...?"

"My employer. I worked for the Freret family."

"You were their housekeeper?"

"Nanny. I took care of their children."

"That was the job you had before you came here."

"Yes."

"Why didn't you look for another nanny job?"

"Leaving the children after all those years... It wasn't easy. I didn't want to go through that again."

"Why did you leave?"

"The youngest was about to start school, and they didn't need me anymore." That was almost true. The Frerets would have dismissed her when their youngest daughter, Nicole, started school. The fiasco with Etienne had only hastened her departure by a few months.

"That must have been tough. Do you keep in touch?"

"No."

Travis raised an eyebrow, but didn't press the point. He must think it was strange that the children didn't correspond. She did. Their desertion hurt almost as much as Etienne's betrayal.

"What happened between you and Etienne?"

"We were engaged. It was a very short engagement."

"Why? Because you figured out you weren't in love with him?"

"No. He broke it off, not me. The Frerets didn't approve of me. They convinced Etienne to end the engagement."

"Aha! That's why you didn't have a reference from them. Except for glowing recommendations from your teachers and the employment agency, your résumé was a little sketchy. So the Frerets were a bunch of snobs, so what? You're better off without them. And him."

"I know that. I thought you said your mother was a snob, too."

"She's recently developed tendencies in that direction. We can tease her out of them. We only have to point out that her family and the Rules come from a long line of dirt farmers."

"You tease a lot, don't you?"

"Only family and friends. We are friends, you know. Cindy—"

"Travis," she interrupted. "I know I promised, but I don't think I can stay here, after…"

"After I took advantage of you when you were hurting. My only excuse is—hell, I don't have one. The truth is, I want you, Cindy. You must know that now. And for a while there, I thought the feeling was mutual."

"I don't know what I want. I thought I'd learned all I needed to know about men from Etienne. I was wrong. I don't have a clue. All I'm sure of is that I can't make another mistake."

"But, Cindy—"

"I mean it. I'm not making another stupid mistake like I did with Etienne."

"You aren't stupid. You trusted the wrong man."

"I did more than that. I—never mind. Please release me from my promise. I can't stay here."

"Forget about the promise. Think about your own self-interest. You want to start a business. That takes money, always more money than you think it will. I'll give you a bonus if you stay until my birthday."

"A bonus?"

"A substantial bonus. And I'll give you a few pointers on how to get started in the business world."

Cindy's heart began beating faster. She could learn

a lot from Travis. How much would he share? And what would he expect in return? ''Pointers?'' she asked, her eyes narrowed.

''Lessons. Whatever you need to know. You'll have an MBA from the Rule School of Business before I'm finished with you.''

A pinprick of guilt deflated her excitement. ''That's too much. I feel like I'm blackmailing you. You have guests coming, and I did promise I wouldn't leave.''

Travis leaned back in his chair and gave her a stern look. ''First lesson, Cindy. Supply and demand. You've got what I need, and right now you're the only game in town. That means you can set your own terms. That is not a crime, it's shrewd business. I'm willing to pay you for your time and effort in money, and in knowledge.''

''Supply and demand, hmm? I like the sound of that. All right, Mr. Rule, you've got a deal.'' She stuck out her hand.

Travis reached across the table, took her hand and held it for a few seconds before giving it a firm shake. ''Good. Now, get some rest, and we'll talk again in the morning.'' He got up and began picking up the dishes.

''I should clean up in here.''

''I'll do it. Go.''

''You sure are bossy,'' Cindy said. But she smiled when she said it. She had a reason to stay at the Monarch Ranch. Two reasons—a bonus, and knowledge she couldn't buy with money.

''I am the boss. Don't you forget it. Be in my office for your first lesson promptly at eight.''

''Yes, sir, Professor Rule. Good night.'' She smiled at him again.

\* \* \*

Travis watched Cindy trail off to her bedroom, feeling as if he'd just negotiated a labor contract with the Teamsters, instead of with one feisty housekeeper. A successful negotiation—she had agreed to stick around for a while longer. And she'd smiled at him. Twice.

Next step, convince Cindy to sign a lifetime contract as his wife.

That would be quite a feat. Cindy's experience with Breaux—and he had a strong feeling there was more to that story—had obviously made her wary of men, and marriage. And he was planning to win her heart with lessons on income forecasting and cost accounting? Travis groaned. While his mother and her two candidates for daughter-in-law watched?

Maybe he wasn't so smart, after all.

He felt better the next morning. A good night's rest had gone a long way toward restoring his battered confidence. After breakfast Travis waited for Cindy in his office. She arrived promptly at eight.

"Sit at the desk, Cindy. I'll pace. I think better when I move around."

Cindy took her seat, picked up the pen he'd left lying by a legal pad and looked at him expectantly.

"So you want to be an entrepreneur, Miss Ellerbee?"

"Yes, I do."

"Tell me your plan."

A tiny frown appeared between her eyebrows, making her look serious and adorable at the same time. "I'm going to open a needlework shop. I plan to teach classes in knitting, crocheting, petit point, and so forth, and I'll sell supplies, too. The name of the shop will be Golden Pins and Silver Needles.''

''Too long.''

''Excuse me?''

''The name is too long. People remember short and snappy. Word of mouth is important for small businesses with limited advertising budgets. Pins and Needles, perhaps. Go on. What kind of supplies are you going to sell?''

''Pins and needles, of course. And yarn, embroidery thread, pattern books, instruction books, kits, cotton material for quilting—''

''Have you looked in the San Antonio telephone book? I have one here.''

''N-no.''

''I did, last night. The Yellow Pages list several quilt shops, and one or two needlework shops. You should visit them. See what you can offer that they don't. You may decide not to compete with the quilt stores, for example.'' He looked over her shoulder as she wrote ''visit stores'' on the legal pad.

''No quilts? I like quilts.'' She didn't look happy or convinced.

Travis's confidence began to waver. Poking holes in her dream might not be the best way to show Cindy how lovable he was. ''That was only an example. We don't have enough information about the market to decide that issue now. What about suppliers?''

''Suppliers?'' she asked.

''Have you located sources for the materials you will sell? Knitting yarn, embroidery thread, bolts of cotton?''

''Yes. That's one thing I did think of.'' She looked

relieved. "I've gotten catalogs from several whole-salers."

"And you've compared prices, talked to salesmen, asked about discounts?"

"N-no. Discounts?"

"Most suppliers have some kind of discount policy. They don't necessarily tell you about it, however. You have to ask."

"I haven't talked to any of the suppliers yet. It seemed a little premature."

"It's never too soon to ask questions. The suppliers may know things you need to know. If you ask the right questions, you may learn about your potential competitors, for example. Or maybe a supplier has been trying to get his products into San Antonio, where one of his competitors has a lock on the market. He may be willing to give you deep discounts just to get a foothold in the area."

Scribbling furiously, Cindy muttered, "I don't know anything about business."

Travis stopped pacing and stood in front of the desk. "You will," he promised, resisting the urge to lean down and give her an encouraging kiss.

"I can never repay you for what you're doing—"

"Sure you can. Embroider more crowns on my shirts." He walked over to the fax machine. "Now, let's look at the leasing information my staff dug up. They've got everything from regional and strip malls to downtown storefronts, to neighborhood outlets. I'll show you how to do a cost comparison. First, we need to figure out the square footage—"

The phone on the desk rang. Cindy picked up the receiver. "Monarch Ranch." After a pause, she said,

"One moment, please." Holding her hand over the mouthpiece, she said, "It's your brother."

Travis took the phone from her. "Yeah?"

"Travis? Treat. Thought you'd like an advance warning. Mom's leaving for the ranch first thing in the morning."

"Flying?"

"Nope. Driving. Mom wanted me to fly them down this afternoon, but I told her I couldn't leave my post as acting CEO." He paused. "She actually believed that. Told me how nice it was that I was finally showing some ambition. Anyway, she decided they would drive down instead. They should get there around noon."

"Damn. I need more time—"

"Time? Time for what?"

"None of your business."

"Okay, no reason to bite my head off. Who answered the telephone, by the way?"

"Cindy Ellerbee. The housekeeper."

"Oh. I thought maybe one of your women had tracked you to your lair. I forgot about the housekeeper."

"Thanks for the heads-up. I'll talk to you later."

Travis hung up the telephone. Brooke and Stephanie. He needed time with Cindy, not with them. His mother had invited them to stay at the ranch until his birthday. He had to get rid of them, but how?

"Is anything wrong?"

"Yeah. That was Treat. Mom and Stephanie and Brooke are on their way here."

Frowning, Cindy asked, "What's wrong with that? I thought you were expecting them."

"I won't have as much time for lessons."

"We could forget about the driving lessons," Cindy said, her soft lips curving into a sly smile.

"No. You might need a delivery truck for your business, one with a standard shift. I'll find time for you, don't worry."

She stood up and walked to the door. "I'll get the guest rooms ready. Your mother will want the master suite?"

Travis followed her out of the office and up the stairs. "Yeah. I'll help. We don't have much time."

"When are they arriving? Tonight?" Cindy gathered sheets and blankets from the linen closet.

Travis took them from her and carried them to the master bedroom. "No, tomorrow. Around noon. How are we fixed for groceries? Will we need to make a trip to Carrizo before they get here?"

"We could use some more fresh fruit and vegetables. I knew I should have planted a kitchen garden. But when it was only me, it didn't seem worth the effort."

"We'll drive into town first thing in the morning. You can drive. That way we'll get in one more lesson before the guests arrive."

"I don't know. Maybe I should stay here. The library could use another dusting." Cindy finished making up the bed and headed for the guest rooms.

"The library is fine. I need you to go with me. I don't know what to buy."

"All right. I can vacuum and dust this afternoon. Which rooms do you want to use?"

"We'll put Brooke in the blue room, and Stephanie can use the room across the hall." But not for long, he hoped. What would make them leave? Quickly?

He stopped, transfixed. What if he told Brooke and

Stephanie he was going to test them on their wifely attributes? If Cindy was right, they would be so insulted, they'd be out the door and on the way back to San Antonio before his mother could stop them. "I'll leave you to it," he told Cindy. "I've got to take care of some business."

Travis retreated to his office, a satisfied smile on his face. This could work, he thought. Not only to scare off his unwanted guests, but to keep other predatory women at bay, too.

Brooke and Stephanie would talk. He could count on that. They would spread the word that Travis Rule had gone crazy. He could hear the buzz. Testing for a wife? What kind of idiot would do such a thing? Oh, he still has money, but how long will it last? Psychiatrists are expensive. And a crazy man can't run a successful business.

Business. Travis drew his brows together in a frown.

Would being thought of as eccentric, or just plain nuts, be bad for RuleCo? Not necessarily, he decided after a few minutes' thought. If his competitors thought he'd lost it, they could make the mistake of underestimating him. He could live with that.

Anyway he looked at it, this was a win-win situation. He would be alone again with Cindy in a matter of hours, and he'd be free of wannabe wives until after he had the one he wanted.

## 6

$\longrightarrow \!\!\! \longleftarrow$

Cindy had just finished putting away the last of the groceries when she heard a car in the driveway. She tucked a loose strand of hair back into the bun at the nape of her neck, straightened her apron and headed for the front door.

Travis got there before her. He opened the door, and three women entered the foyer. Two of them were young, blond and beautiful. The candidates for marriage, Cindy thought, with a sudden sinking feeling in the pit of her stomach. She'd almost forgotten the reason for their visit.

Why Travis's hunt for a wife should make her queasy, she could not begin to fathom. Unless she resented the time he would be spending with them, time she wanted Travis to spend with her. To give her lessons. In business.

Cindy squelched her envious thoughts and turned her attention to the third woman. She recognized her right away from the photos in the library. She was Travis's mother. Sally Rule had salt-and-pepper hair, a trim figure and a smile that lit up the room. Her photographs didn't do her justice. She entered first, hugged Travis and kissed him on the cheek.

"Travis, dear. How nice to see you! You know Brooke and Stephanie."

The two women came in side by side. "Hello, Travis," said the first one, shaking his hand. "Travis, darling," murmured the second one, her voice breathy. She kissed him on the cheek, but only because he turned his head at the last moment. The woman had definitely been aiming for his mouth.

The sinking feeling faded, replaced by another stronger emotion. Before Cindy could identify what it was, Mrs. Rule caught sight of her hovering in the background.

"And who is this?" she asked, smiling warmly.

"Cindy. Miss Ellerbee. The housekeeper," said Travis. "Cindy, this is my mother."

Mrs. Rule advanced on Cindy and gave her a quick hug. "So nice to meet you. You came highly recommended. I hope this crowd won't be too much for you."

Flustered by the show of affection, Cindy murmured, "N-no, of course not. I'm pleased to meet you, too, Mrs. Rule." Why had Travis said his mother was a snob?

"Call me Sal. Everyone does." She turned back to the trio in the doorway. "Come on in, girls. Cindy, our guests are Brooke Bennett and Stephanie Lord."

The first blonde—Brooke—smiled and nodded. Stephanie kept her gaze trained on Travis, looking for another opportunity to kiss him, Cindy thought with a sniff.

"Travis, would you get the luggage out of the car?" asked Sal. "I left the keys in the ignition. Which rooms have you put us in, Cindy? I'd like to freshen up, and I'm sure Brooke and Stephanie feel the same way.'' She started up the stairs. ''Don't worry about lunch, by the way. We stopped in Pearsall and had a bite. Am I in the master suite?'' she asked when the procession reached the top of the stairs.

''Yes, ma'am,'' said Cindy.

''Not 'ma'am,' dear. Sal,'' she corrected. Sal turned left, heading down the hall that contained the family's rooms. When she reached the door to the master suite, she stopped and said, ''Do you know what, girls? I'm feeling a little tired. I think I'll take a nap while you're unpacking and settling in.'' She looked over her shoulder. ''I'm sure you two will find something to amuse yourselves with, won't you?''

The two blondes murmured their agreement.

''Follow me, and I'll show you to your rooms.'' Cindy led them to the guest wing.

They were outside the room Travis had designated for Brooke when he appeared with the luggage. ''Which ones are yours, Brooke?'' he asked.

Brooke pointed to one of the suitcases. ''That one's mine.''

''I'll bring it in,'' said Travis, following Brooke into her room. He left the other three bags in the hall.

Cindy led Stephanie to the bedroom across the hall. ''This is your room, Miss Lord.'' She turned to leave.

''Wait just a minute,'' Stephanie said, her voice curt.

Cindy stopped. ''Yes?''

''What was your name again?''

''Cindy Ellerbee.''

''How quaint,'' sneered Stephanie. ''Well, Ellerbee. Run me a bath. I'm all dusty from the trip.''

Gritting her teeth at the woman's rude commands,

Cindy went into the guest room's adjoining bath and turned on the water. Stephanie remained in the bedroom, standing by the bed. Cindy kept one eye on the water level in the tub, and the other on Stephanie. The petite blonde had a calculating look about her. What was she up to?

Stephanie began hurriedly unbuttoning her blouse. She shrugged out of the garment just as Travis entered with her suitcases.

"Oops, sorry," he said, dropping the suitcases.

"Oh, my," said Stephanie, holding the blouse in front of her, but not high enough to cover her lacy demi-bra. "Naughty boy, sneaking up on me like this."

"I should have knocked, but the door was open..."

Why didn't he leave? fumed Cindy. And why couldn't he tear his gaze away from Stephanie's chest? More to the point, why did she care?

Cindy turned off the water and walked into the bedroom. "Your bath is ready, Miss Lord."

Stephanie ignored her. "I'll be down as soon as I bathe and change, Travis. Will you be waiting for me?" she asked archly.

"For you and Brooke. I've already told her—I want to see both of you in the library as soon as you're ready."

"I'll hurry," breathed Stephanie.

"No rush," said Travis, leaving the room.

As soon as he was gone, Stephanie turned to Cindy. "Well, what are you standing there for? Unpack my bags. There's a yellow sundress—get it out and if it needs pressing, see to it. And hurry. I don't want to be late for the meeting with Travis." She stripped off the rest of her clothes and tossed them to Cindy.

"Take care of these, too, Ellerbee." She disappeared into the bathroom.

Cindy, feeling like a servant for the first time in six months, did as she was told. After she returned the freshly pressed sundress to Stephanie, she stopped by Brooke's room to see if she needed assistance.

Pulling on jeans, Brooke smiled. "No, thanks. I've already unpacked. I only brought jeans and shirts, for the most part. This is a ranch, after all. From all the luggage, I'd say Stephanie packed her complete designer wardrobe."

Cindy returned her smile. "Yes, Miss Bennett. She did bring quite a few clothes with her."

"Brooke, please. And may I call you Cindy?"

"Of course. Would you like me to show you to the library?"

"Yes, thank you. I've known Travis and his family for ages, but I've never been invited to the ranch before."

Cindy led Brooke to the library. She started upstairs to see if Stephanie needed directions, but then stopped. From what she'd seen, she already knew which of the two women Travis would choose, if he decided to marry before his birthday. Not that she cared, she insisted, willing her stomach to unknot itself. Travis Rule's marital status did not affect her in any way.

Except Travis had said they were friends. Friends looked out for one another, didn't they? As a friend, she would leave him alone with Brooke for a little longer—enough time to counter any unfair advantage Stephanie had gained with her calculated little striptease.

Cindy's noble motives evaporated like smoke when

Stephanie appeared at the top of the stairs. Who was she kidding? She plain didn't like the woman.

Looking down her nose, Stephanie said, "Ellerbee, where have you been? I tried ringing for you, but there's no intercom system."

"No, Miss Lord."

"Well, find a bell or a buzzer or something I can use to call you with. I'm not searching all over for you every time I need assistance. What are you standing there for? Come here."

Cindy walked to the top of the stairs. "How may I help you?"

"Look down the front of my dress."

"Excuse me?"

"I said, look down the front of my dress. Can you tell I'm not wearing a bra?"

"No, miss. The neckline's low, but it's not gaping."

"Damn." Stephanie crossed her arms under her breasts and leaned forward. "How about now?"

"Oh, yes." Cindy was shocked in spite of herself. The woman wanted Travis to see her naked breasts!

"Good. Has Brooke gone down already?"

"Yes. She's in the library with Mr. Rule."

"Take me there, and hurry. That little witch is probably all over him by now."

"The library is this way." She hurried to the library and left Stephanie with Brooke and Travis, resisting the temptation to stand outside the library with her eye glued to the keyhole.

The trio could have an orgy for all she cared.

Travis, sitting behind the desk, steepled his fingers and contemplated the two women. B.C.—before

Cindy—he wouldn't have faulted his mother's choices. Both were petite blondes. Both were intelligent and well educated. He knew from past acquaintance that they both held responsible positions in their respective family businesses.

They weren't peas in a pod, though. Brooke was lightly tanned, and her dark blond hair was short and breezy looking. She looked athletic and wholesome, like the girl next door. He approved of the jeans and shirt she'd changed into—she looked like she belonged on a ranch.

Stephanie looked more like a fashion model than a cowgirl.

Her fair complexion and pale blond hair gave her a golden, expensive look. The silky dress she wore left very little to the imagination. As Treat had said, both women had all the right equipment to turn a man on.

Stephanie flaunted hers.

He cleared his throat. "Stephanie. Brooke. I see no need to beat around the bush. We all know why you're here. My mother expects me to choose one of you to be my wife."

"Really?" said Brooke, with a cheeky grin.

"I had no idea," said Stephanie.

"Can the crap, ladies, or you're both out of the running. I have certain basic requirements, and the most basic is that my future bride be honest to a fault."

"Now that you mention it, your mother did tell me about the Rule family tradition," said Brooke, still grinning cheerfully.

"Yes. She told me the story, too," Stephanie admitted. "You have to get married before your thirty-fifth birthday."

"According to the family tradition. Now. Here's the plan. I've come up with a series of tests which will demonstrate whether or not you meet my needs. You'll each take the tests, and whoever scores the highest gets Great-Grandmother Rule's engagement ring. And me."

"Tests? What kind of tests?" asked Brooke. "I thought we were just going to spend time together, get to know one another."

"Tests. What fun! When do we start?" said Stephanie, hugging herself in apparent glee. She leaned forward, giving him an excellent view down the front of her dress. Stephanie had dispensed with the sexy bra she'd made sure he'd seen her wearing earlier. Like he'd thought before, she was a woman who didn't mind showing off her charms.

"Right away. First, I want you each to write an essay about marriage—what you expect from me as your husband and why you would make me a good wife." That was the only test he'd come up with, and the only one he'd need.

"An essay? This is a joke, right?" said Brooke. She'd stopped grinning.

"How many words?" asked Stephanie.

"No joke, and no word limit." He stood up, frowning. Brooke didn't look pleased, but she hadn't gotten up and walked out. Stephanie appeared calm and businesslike. Neither woman had reacted the way he'd expected. "You'll find paper and pens on the library table," he said lamely.

"An essay? You really want us to write an essay?"

Brooke asked. Now she sounded disgusted. Maybe she, at least, would leave.

"You can always drop out of the competition," said Stephanie.

Brooke glared at her. "And leave you a clear field? No way. I never quit before the buzzer sounds. Where's that paper?"

"How long do we have?" asked Stephanie.

Travis looked at his watch. He was disgusted, if they weren't. What kind of women would put up with being tested for marriage? "It's almost two. You can have until five. That should give you plenty of time. When you're finished, join me in the living room. We'll have drinks before dinner."

He left them to it and went straight to the kitchen.

Standing in front of the sink, Cindy was up to her elbows in suds.

"What are you doing? Did the dishwasher conk out?"

"No. I'm washing the crystal and the china. It's too delicate for the dishwasher."

He leaned against the counter. "I'm in trouble."

"What kind of trouble?"

"Our guests. My mother's matchmaking."

"Your mother seems very nice. I'm sure she is only doing this for your own good. She doesn't want you to spend the rest of your life a lonely and bitter man."

"Lonely and bitter? I don't think so. All alone and happy as a clam, more likely," he muttered. "I'm sorry. I'm not feeling very hospitable today. I wish they hadn't come."

"You're not happy with your mother's choices?"

Wishful thinking had him believing Cindy sounded

pleased about that. "No. Help me think up a way to get rid of them. I thought I had one, but it didn't work."

"You're teasing, right? Why would you want them to leave? Brooke and Stephanie are both very pretty." Cindy wouldn't look at him, he noticed. She seemed fascinated by the soap bubbles in the sink.

"Yep. Not a plain-Jane in the bunch." He went to the refrigerator and opened it. Could it be Cindy was jealous of Brooke and Stephanie? "Do we have any margarita mix?"

"In the freezer. Where are they?"

"Who?"

"*Your* guests."

"In the library, writing essays."

"Essays?"

"Yeah. A variation on Mom's contest idea. I gave them three hours. I told them to meet me in the living room at five for cocktails. We have time for another driving lesson now, if you'd like. You did very well this morning, by the way."

"Thanks, but I don't have time for a lesson now. I've got too much to do. They actually agreed to write essays about why they want to marry you? Both of them?"

"Yes." He smiled, wickedly pleased that Cindy couldn't keep from asking about Brooke and Stephanie. "I didn't limit them to twenty-five words, though."

"Why would you? They could probably write volumes."

"Are you being sarcastic?" His grin broadened. She *was* jealous. Maybe he should keep Brooke and Stephanie around for a day or two. He hadn't considered what seeing other women fight—compete—over him might do to Cindy. "Volumes?"

She sniffed. "If they agreed to write essays, they must have reasons. Lots of them. They really weren't insulted?"

"No, not at all. Oh, Brooke seemed a little taken aback, but Stephanie was a trooper from the beginning." He returned the margarita mix to the freezer. "I'll fix drinks later. Now I think I'll go check on Mom. If she's awake, I'll bring her up to speed. She may have an idea for test number two. See you later."

He bounded up the stairs, whistling. If Brooke and Stephanie didn't come to their senses after test number one, he'd better be ready with another, something even more eccentric than essays on marriage. Fingering the embroidered crown on his chest, he smiled. He knew exactly what to do for a second test. He was in his room, getting ready for test number two when his mother joined him.

"What are you doing?" she asked.

"Tearing holes in my shirts."

"I can see that. Whatever for?"

"Test number two. Mending."

"Tests? What are you up to, Travis?"

"I'm following your advice. And Treat's. I'm testing Brooke and Stephanie on their qualifications to be my wife. Right now they're writing essays on why they want to marry me."

"Travis! That was a joke." His mother had the grace to look horrified. That was how Brooke and Stephanie should have reacted.

"Trust me. They're not laughing, Mom."

She reached up and touched his forehead. "Do you

feel all right? Perhaps you'd better go into town and see Dr. Frazier.''

''I never felt better.'' Planting a kiss on her cheek, he told her, ''I'm doing my best to beat the deadline, Mom. I thought you'd be happy.''

''I want *you* to be happy. That's why I've pushed so hard for you to settle down and start your own family. But I'm not sure testing women is a good idea—''

''Better than good. Brilliant.''

''And the next test is mending? Why?''

''Mending is very important.''

His mother looked him over, her gaze coming to rest on his chest. ''That's an unusual design on your shirt pocket. It looks like the Monarch brand.''

''It is. Cindy embroidered it to cover up a hole.''

''Hmm. That was nice of her. You and she seem to have become very friendly.''

''Not nearly friendly enough, Mom. Not nearly friendly enough.''

Brooke entered the kitchen a few minutes after four. She looked disgruntled, Cindy thought.

''I can't find Travis. Do you know where he is? I need to hand in…this.''

''The last time I saw him, he was going to talk to his mother,'' Cindy told her, eyeing the single page of paper Brooke held in her hand. ''Finished already?''

''Yes, such as it is,'' Brooke said. ''Travis told you about the essay contest?'' She looked embarrassed.

Nodding, Cindy said, ''It was his mother's idea, I think.''

''I knew she was anxious for him to marry.''

"So I heard."

"You would. Servants know everything." She turned red. "I'm sorry, forget I said that."

"I'm not ashamed of being a servant."

"I can see that. And there's no reason you should be. I meant I'm sorry for making it sound like you'd been eavesdropping."

"Oh, I see. Apology accepted. Can I get you something to drink?"

"How about a shot of hemlock? Just kidding. I'm having a little trouble adjusting to this situation. Don't you find it strange?"

"Very strange."

"Good. I was beginning to feel like Alice down the rabbit hole. Having Mrs. Rule act as a...a procurer for her son was weird enough, but tests? This gets screwier and screwier. I've never heard that insanity runs in the Rule family, but I'm beginning to wonder. I wish I'd never agreed—I'm sorry. You don't want to hear about my problems."

Oh, but she did. "Don't you want to marry Travis—Mr. Rule?"

"No. Maybe. I don't know." Brooke sat down at the kitchen table. "The truth is, Cindy, I'm in love with someone else. I'd marry him in a minute, if he'd have me. But he won't."

"Why not?" She bit her lip. "Now it's my turn to apologize. That's none of my business."

"I've kind of made it your business, haven't I?" Brooke asked ruefully. "I'm rich. Very rich. He isn't. And he's made it painfully clear he'll never marry me until his net worth matches or tops mine. That could take forever. I'm twenty-nine. I want a husband and children, and I don't want to wait until I'm too old to enjoy them. And my parents always said money should marry money—they don't approve of Joe, and he feels the same way about them. So when Mrs. Rule told me about Travis's problem and asked me to visit..."

"You accepted."

"Right. I've always liked Travis. And he is The Richest Bachelor in Texas, so he would meet with my family's approval. But I didn't know there would be *tests.*" She stood up. "I think I'll go for a walk. Give Travis my essay, will you, please?"

"Sure."

Forty-five minutes later, Stephanie appeared in the doorway, holding several pages of paper. "Here you are. Have you found me a bell yet?"

"Only this one." Cindy held up a large cowbell. "It was in the garage."

Stephanie took it. "It will have to do. Have you seen Brooke and Travis? They both seem to have disappeared."

"Miss Bennett went for a walk. I haven't seen Travis—Mr. Rule lately."

"Oh, well, as long as they're not together. Get me a glass of water, will you?"

Cindy turned on the faucet.

"Not tap water. Perrier. Or another brand."

"We don't have bottled water, Miss Lord."

"Never mind, then." She looked at the diamond-encrusted watch on her wrist. "I'll wait for cocktails. Tell me, Ellerbee, how long has Travis been here?"

"Only a few days."

"Just the two of you?"

"Yes, Miss Lord."

"But he has been here before."

"No, miss. That is, this is the first visit he's made to the ranch since I've been here."

"How long have you known him? Where did you meet?"

"Excuse me? Meet who?"

"Cut the innocent act, Ellerbee. Travis Rule, of course. Your...employer." She slanted a sly look at Cindy. "He's been out of circulation for almost a year. I knew he had to have a...companion stashed somewhere. I never thought of the ranch, though. Isn't it rather inconvenient?"

Finally grasping the woman's meaning, Cindy could only gape at her in shock.

"Don't look so dismayed, Ellerbee. I won't tell." She left, taking the cowbell and her essay with her, and leaving Cindy feeling more than insulted. She'd been violated. What a nasty woman! She should have told her to take her suspicions and—

With a moan, Cindy sat down at the kitchen table. She hadn't had the presence of mind to deny Stephanie's sordid accusation, much less to tell her off. The truth was, she was as ill equipped to defend herself against lies now as she had been six months ago.

At least this time no one would believe the charge, if Stephanie decided to make it public. It was too absurd. And easily refuted. Travis would deny that they were involved. No one would question his word. He might be The Richest Bachelor in Texas, but he also had a reputation of being scrupulously honest.

Cindy chewed her bottom lip. Travis had a way of infuriating her, but she couldn't help worrying about him. If he went through with his crazy plan, it looked like he would end with a woman in love with someone else or with a woman who loved only herself.

He deserved better.

With a sigh Cindy got up and began setting the dining room table for four. Travis Rule and his future wife, if any, were no concern of hers. As for Stephanie, the best she could hope for was that the woman would become so involved with the contest that she wouldn't have time for insulting the hired help.

After dinner Travis disappeared upstairs with the two essays, and the three women adjourned to the family room to watch television. Cindy cleared the table. She had dried the last crystal goblet when Mrs. Rule joined her in the kitchen.

"Need any help, Cindy?"

"Oh, no, ma'am—Sal. Thank you."

"Are you sure cooking and cleaning for four people won't be too much for you? We can always hire someone else to help out for a day or two."

"That won't be necessary. I've had no one to look after for almost six months. This is a treat for me."

"Treat? Is he here?" Travis walked into the kitchen. His hair was rumpled and his eyes were bleary.

"No, dear. Have you finished reading the essays?" asked his mother.

"Yes."

"Well, don't keep us in suspense. Who won?"

"Stephanie, I guess. She waxed poetic about family, togetherness and children. All Brooke said was money should marry money."

"I'm surprised. Brooke never struck me as a woman who put money before everything else."

Cindy bit her tongue to keep from telling them that Brooke had her reasons. It wasn't her secret to tell. She might think Brooke would be a better wife for

Travis than Stephanie—how could she think otherwise after the way Stephanie had behaved toward her?—but it wasn't her decision to make. Nevertheless, she couldn't help preferring Brooke. Once she married Travis, it was possible, even probable, that Brooke would fall out of love with Joe and into love with her husband.

But after one test, Stephanie Lord was ahead on points. That didn't bear thinking about.

"Cindy?" Travis tapped her on the shoulder, making her jump. "I need some supplies for the next test."

"Yes? What?"

"Needles and thread. And scissors. Anything else, Mom?"

"Those two shirts you mutilated. You'll never guess the next test, Cindy. Mending. Which reminds me—the petit point cushion on my chaise longue has been repaired. Did you do that?"

Cindy nodded. "I hope you don't mind."

"Mind? I love that cushion. My mother made it, and one of my husband's hounds chewed the corner off. Thank you so much, dear. You certainly sew a fine seam. Not many young women today are capable of that kind of workmanship."

Blushing, Cindy smiled at Sal.

"Cindy wants to open her own needlework shop," Travis said. "In one of the big cities in Texas. So, is repairing needlepoint a rare skill?"

"It certainly is." Sal nodded. "Well, Cindy, I hope you choose San Antonio for your shop. I'll be a regular customer."

"Thank you. I'll get the supplies now." Cindy left Travis and his mother in the kitchen while she gathered thread and needles. She was fairly glowing with pride. Mrs. Rule was exactly the kind of woman she'd always wanted for a mother.

She stopped, stricken. She'd done it again—fallen into her old habit of looking for a family of her very own. She'd never be part of the Rule family. She was too old to be adopted. As for the other way to join a family…

Travis had teased her, and he'd kissed her once or twice. Kisses weren't proposals. Not that she wanted him to propose. She didn't love him. She had begun to like him, a little. He had taken care of her when she needed help with the cactus thorns, although he hadn't been above taking advantage of the situation. But he had apologized and generously offered to share his business knowledge.

On the other hand, what kind of man tested women for marriage? She wasn't sure she even liked him much anymore.

Not that it mattered. She didn't have to like him to learn from him. She forced her thoughts away from Travis and back to the future she'd planned for herself during the long months she'd happily spent alone.

San Antonio would be perfect for her needlework shop. But she wouldn't like a mall, no matter how the rents compared to other locations. She would live in a few tiny rooms above her store, just as she'd envisioned. Her living room would have a plump, overstuffed chair and ottoman with a good lamp next to it, the perfect spot to curl up with a good book or a cross-stitch project. She would have gleaming copper pots and pans hanging from a rack in the kitchen, and a four-poster bed in the bedroom, covered with a quilt she'd made herself.

Sal would be her best customer, and she'd recommend Cindy's store to all her wealthy friends. She would also be sure to keep Cindy informed about Travis and his wife and children.

Cindy frowned. Did she really want to hear about Travis for the rest of her life? She didn't think so.

Dallas might be a better place for her shop, after all.

Gathering up the last of the supplies, she returned to the kitchen. Mrs. Rule had left, and she was alone with Travis. She handed him two small baskets. "Here. I put needles and several shades of thread in each basket, along with a pincushion and scissors. Will that be all?"

He poked around in the baskets. "Looks fine to me."

"When is the next test?"

"Tomorrow morning."

"Do they know?"

"Yeah. I told them over dinner. Brooke looked relieved—she must know how to sew. Steph turned a little green."

"I hope it wasn't my cooking."

"I don't think so. She had seconds of everything. Amazing how some people can eat anything they want and not lose their figures. Anyway, while they're out of the way and busily sewing, we can look at that lease information. I'll meet you in my office after breakfast tomorrow."

Travis walked out of the kitchen carrying the baskets, and Cindy retreated to her room.

She'd been asleep long enough to begin dreaming, when an urgent knock sounded on her door. Groggily, she sat up. Yawning sleepily, she sat up. "Who is it? Travis?"

The door opened, and Stephanie walked in, switching on the ceiling light. "Does Travis make a habit of visiting you late at night?"

Blinking at the sudden light, Cindy yawned again. "Of course not. I didn't hear the bell. What do you want?"

"That bell would wake the dead. This is between you and me." She closed the door behind her. Stephanie had her basket with her, Cindy noticed. "I want you to sew up the hole in this shirt. I'll give you a hundred dollars."

"No. That wouldn't be fair."

"Fair? I'll tell you what's unfair. Brooke knows how to darn. When we were alone in the family room, she told me that her grandmother taught her how when she was a kid. She thinks she's got this test locked. Two hundred dollars."

"No."

"Listen, you little…housekeeper. Help me out, or you can forget about this cushy job. Once I'm Mrs. Travis Rule, you're out of here. Do this one little thing, and I'll see to it that you have a lifetime position. You can even keep on sleeping with the boss."

"I am not sleeping with Travis, and I am not helping you cheat. Please leave my room."

Stephanie glared at her. "Where did you say you worked before this? You'd better plan on going back there. You won't be here for long."

"I'm aware of that." She had her own plan, and it certainly didn't involve returning to the Frerets, or staying at the Monarch Ranch forever. "Get out, Stephanie."

"I'm going. But I won't forget this. You'll be sorry you didn't help me, little Miss Cinderella. I get even with people who cross me."

# 7

Travis strode purposefully into the kitchen around ten o'clock the next morning. Cindy looked up from the cookbook she'd been reading, noting absently that he was wearing jeans and the shirt she'd mended for him. He'd been wearing that shirt a lot lately. She'd had to wash and iron it several times.

Of course, two of his shirts were now in the hands of the wannabe brides. Still, he had to have more than three shirts. He was The Richest Bachelor in Texas, after all. It had to be a guy thing. She'd seen other males develop an irrational bond with an article of clothing. Little Robert Freret had insisted on wearing the same ratty pajamas for months, not giving them up until they'd disintegrated beyond repair.

"Come on, Cindy, time to get down to business."

"Business?" The last thing she wanted was to be alone with Travis this morning. She'd dreamed about him again last night, a disturbing dream that had begun with Travis kissing her with his too-tempting mouth until she forgot all about living alone and liking it. But her romantic dream had not ended happily—the last image before waking had been Travis slipping a diamond engagement ring on another woman's finger.

Her subconscious needed to give up on romance. At least when she was awake she didn't waste time wishing for things she'd never have. She knew a man like Travis would never fall in love with someone like her. Which was far from a tragedy. Any man who would test women for marriage was not the—

She realized suddenly that Travis was waiting patiently for a response from her. "No, thank you. I really don't have time.... The guests. Your mother..."

"You've washed the breakfast dishes. Lunch isn't for hours. Brooke and Stephanie are busily mending, and Mom went over to the Ortegas to see baby Hector. After that, she's going to the bunkhouse to give Gus and the boys a hard time. Face it, Cindy, your morning is free. Go on and change out of that uniform and meet me out front. We'll try the Bronco today."

"Driving? I thought you were talking about business."

"We'll do both. You'll drive, and I'll talk about profit and loss—how to maximize the former and minimize the latter."

Grumbling under her breath, Cindy went to her room and pulled on a pair of jeans and a cotton sweater. She glanced in the mirror over the dresser on her way out of the room. She looked pale. Pinching her cheeks, she grumbled out loud. "No wonder Travis has stayed a bachelor this long! No intelligent woman would have him. Travis Rule is bossy and conceited and...and...I *hate* him!"

She stared at her reflection in the mirror. That seemed a bit strong. She might not approve of the way he'd chosen to find a wife, but *hate?* Where had such a strong emotion come from? A reaction to his imperious commands? A hangover from Stephanie's midnight visit? A desperate longing to be anywhere but the Monarch Ranch?

"Face it, kid. Your dreams aren't the only things turning into nightmares. Lately this job sucks sour lemons." Cindy made a face in the mirror, then twisted her hair into a bun. "But it won't last much longer. Travis's birthday is only a week away. After that, I'm out of here."

Seven days. She could last seven more days, couldn't she? For a substantial bonus? "Darn right!" she told herself. And she would use the time to learn as much as Travis could teach her about running her own business.

Feeling calmer, but still grouchy, Cindy joined Travis in the circular drive at the front of the house.

"What took you so long? And why did you put your hair up? I hate that old-maid hairdo." Travis opened the driver-side door, and Cindy got behind the wheel.

"I'm sorry I kept you waiting, sir. It won't happen again, sir." Cindy pulled the hairpins out of her hair and gave her head a defiant shake. Old maid? Ha! He'd meant that as an insult. She'd show him! A woman could get along without a man—especially a conceited, bossy man—quite nicely. Too bad Brooke and Stephanie didn't realize that. Travis deserved to remain a bachelor for the rest of his life. He wasn't fit to be a husband, not even to one of the terrible twosome.

"That's better. And what's with the 'sir' business?"

Starting the engine, Cindy turned her head and glared at him.

His eyebrows crooked upward. "Never mind. Back out of the driveway this time. We haven't practiced reverse much."

"Yes, sir. Right away, sir." She shifted into reverse and floored the accelerator at the same time she let up on the clutch. She barely missed a date palm at the edge of the driveway.

"Well, hell. You could give Gus ornery lessons this morning. What's got you agitated?"

"Nothing." Cindy managed to ignore Travis and concentrate on driving for all of five minutes. "What's next?" She couldn't help asking. She had to know the next play in the marriage game.

"Parallel parking. We'll have to do that back at the house. I'll line up the Cadillac and Mom's Lexus, and—"

"I am not asking about driving lessons. I want to know what marriage test comes next."

"Oh. That." He sounded distracted. "Watch your speed. These dirt roads aren't race tracks."

Cindy let up on the accelerator. "What examination have you cooked up for your victims today?" For some perverse reason, she couldn't stop thinking about Treat's suggestion, that the final test should be in the bedroom.

"Victims? Are you talking about Brooke and Stephanie?"

She nodded, avoiding his gaze.

"That's not how I would describe them. But, to answer your question, I don't know. I'm hoping a third test won't be necessary."

Cindy jerked her head around and stared at him, steering straight for a fence pole. Travis grabbed the wheel and kept them on the road. "Whoa! Let's stop for a while. I think you need to calm down."

Stopping the car, Cindy gripped the steering wheel and said through clenched teeth, "I'm calm. Why wouldn't I be calm? I don't have any reason to be uncalm."

"Your mind is not on this driving lesson, that's for sure. What's bugging you?"

"Nothing. Not a thing. I am not bugged."

Travis opened the car door and got out. He walked around the front of the car to the driver's side and opened Cindy's door. "Let's walk. I want to check out the windmill at that tank over there." He held out his hand.

Cindy brushed it aside and got out of the car. "I don't need your help," she said nastily.

Holding up his hands like he was being robbed, Travis backed away. "Not even with business? My office faxed some more information about the shops in San Antonio that you would compete with, by the way. We'll go over it when we get back to the house."

Cindy started walking toward the windmill. "Why are you doing this?"

"Doing what?"

"Teaching me to drive a standard shift. Having your employees gather marketing information for me." She took a deep breath. "I mean, it's very nice of you, but—"

"I lo—like you, and I want you to like me."

"Why? What difference could it possibly make to you if I didn't like you? If I hated you?"

"You don't, do you? Hate me?" The shocked expression on his face surprised her. Travis looked worried.

"No. But I don't like what you're doing to Brooke and Stephanie."

"Neither do I." He looked sheepish, then he spoiled it by laughing.

Cindy stopped walking. She turned on Travis, her fists on her hips. "I don't think that's funny. Taking advantage of women who...who..."

"I wasn't laughing at them, Cindy. Trust me, the joke is on me. But there's no need to feel sorry for Brooke or Stephanie. They volunteered for this game."

"Game? Game? Getting married isn't a game. It's your whole life. Yours and...whoever's. And your children's lives. Marriage is *serious.*"

"No kidding? Completely serious? No fun at all?"

Ignoring the playful gleam in his blue eyes, Cindy stormed, "Testing for a wife is cold, calculating and doomed to end in divorce. Or worse!"

"What's worse than divorce?"

"Staying married to someone you don't love, someone who doesn't love you."

"Ah. You think I should love the woman I marry?"

"Yes!"

Leaning negligently against the windmill support, Travis said, "I thought you didn't believe in love."

"I never said that."

"Oh. I must have misunderstood. So, you have been in love?"

"Once," she admitted reluctantly, her indignation fading. "I told you about him."

"Etienne?" A muscle twitched in Travis's jaw, and the teasing gleam faded from his eyes.

"Yes." Why did that feel like a lie? She had loved Etienne, with all her heart.

"What happened?"

"I told you that, too. He didn't love me. And that broke my heart," she insisted, ignoring the steady heartbeats making her feel uncomfortably like a liar once again. "You don't want to hurt Brooke or Stephanie, do you?"

"I'm not going to hurt them. They don't love me. At best they love the idea of being married to The Richest Husband in Texas—second richest, after Jake. Are you still in love with Breaux?"

"No."

"Was Breaux your first lover?" Travis's blue eyes gleamed again, but not like before. He looked anything but playful.

"No! We never—" She folded her arms across her chest. "It's none of your business. I don't want to talk about it."

He moved closer. "You were in love with the guy, and you didn't make love with him?"

Cindy shook her head, refusing to look at him.

"So you're still a virgin?"

"That *really* is none of your business."

He relaxed visibly. "You're still a virgin. And that means you didn't love Breaux. Tell me the whole story, Cindy."

Cindy did not like the look of smug satisfaction on Travis's face. What possible difference could her experience with love or sex make to him? None. She wasn't about to bare her soul to satisfy his prurient curiosity. "I will not. And how dare you question the way I felt about Etienne? I did so love him! Just because I wouldn't...he didn't..."

"Oh, I get it. He didn't love you, and he didn't want you, either?"

"That's not true! He did want me." Enough that he'd lied to get her in his bed.

"Okay. I believe you. To tell you the truth, I can't imagine a man not wanting you. You're very desirable, Cindy." He pushed away from the windmill. "Come here, and I'll show you."

Cindy stayed put, her hands folding into fists. "You are a piece of work, Travis Rule. Thinking every woman you meet is ready to fall into your arms."

"You did," he reminded her, moving closer. "And you kissed me, too. When we were in bed together. Have you forgotten?"

Cindy's knees went mushy. Her brain, too. If it hadn't turned to mush, she would have better sense than to let the heat in his eyes awaken that particular memory. She could feel his hands moving on her naked body, taste that tempting mouth moving on her parted lips. She swayed toward him. "We weren't in bed together. Not that way."

"No. Too bad. It might have been fun." He sounded wistful.

"Fun?" She licked her lips nervously.

"What are you doing, Cindy?" he asked, his eyes on her mouth. "Do you want me to kiss you?"

"N-no. Why would I want that?" Her heart no longer beat with a steady rhythm, and she couldn't seem to fill her lungs with breath.

He tilted her chin up. "Because I do it so well?"

Opening her eyes wide, she pushed his hand away.

"No! You've got a swelled head if you think that, you bossy—"

He stopped her with a kiss. A brief kiss, over almost before she felt his mouth on hers. "I am the boss. And I'm cute, too." Travis grinned at her.

What did he have to be happy about? And why did he want to kiss her? Two women weren't enough for him? Good night, Nellie!

Throwing up her hands, Cindy started walking away from him. Her legs were a bit unsteady, and she couldn't seem to think clearly, but that was easily explained. Sunstroke. She'd been out in the hot Texas sun too long. Certainly not because Travis had kissed her again. That peck he'd planted on her mouth had barely qualified as a kiss, anyway. She would be fine as soon as she got in the shade.

"Wait up, Cindy. We can't go back yet. We haven't come up with another test for Brooke and Stephanie. In case one is needed."

"That is not my problem." She quickened her pace. She didn't have to wait for him—she had the keys. But she couldn't resist letting Travis know how she felt about one thing. "Using your brother's idea would be tacky, though."

"Treat? What did he—oh, yeah. Give the final test in the bedroom. You're right, that would be tacky. Besides, Mom would never let me get away with it. I did have another idea—kids. I thought I could have each of them baby-sit the Ortega brood. Taking care of children is important, don't you think?"

Cindy kept walking. Children? He had to bring up children—the little boys and girls who would call him Daddy and Brooke or Stephanie, Mom. She might not know much about families, but surely this was not the way to make one! Cindy wanted to scream and yell and rage at him, but it wouldn't do any good. Why would he listen to her? No matter what he said, she was only his employee, his student, not his friend.

"Anyway, I called Dolores, but she wouldn't loan me her children. Said I was loco." He opened the truck door for her. "She also mentioned that you were very good with children. You must be, having been a professional nanny. Help me out here, Cindy. Which one of the two contestants do you think would be better with kids?"

"I am not helping you."

"Some friend you are. Here I am, taking the morning to teach you to drive, a friendly thing to do, and you won't return the favor."

"Travis, I—"

"No, that's okay. I'll think of something. Let's go back to the house and see how our two seamstresses are doing."

She tossed him the keys. "You drive. I've had enough for today."

On the way home, Cindy stared blindly at the mesquite trees and cactus. What was happening to her? She'd been angry with Travis, disgusted with his stupid tests, and yet, when he'd touched her lips with his...she'd wanted that tempting mouth on hers for a lot longer than a nanosecond.

It had to be those disturbing dreams. Something in her subconscious would not accept her decision to stay single and keep her heart whole.

Travis stopped the truck in the garage, got out and walked around to open the door for Cindy. When she stepped out of the Bronco, she found herself only a kiss away from Travis.

She had to do it. One kiss. She'd give him one more kiss, and then she'd be cured of this strange need. Placing her hands on his shoulders, Cindy pressed her lips against his tempting mouth, softly at first. What began as a whisper of a kiss quickly flamed into passion. Her hands slid around his neck, her breasts flattened against his chest. She could not get close enough.

Travis must have felt her need. He wrapped his arms around her waist and pulled her tight against his lean, hard body. His lips parted beneath her pleading kiss, and she slipped her tongue inside his hot mouth, tasting him. She kissed the hard line of his jaw, the pulse beating in his throat, a spot beneath his ear, before returning to those tempting lips. As soon as her mouth slanted over his, he took control of the kiss, tangling his tongue with hers, tasting her as deeply as she'd tasted him.

"Travis—oops. Sorry."

Travis jerked his head up, ending the kiss. "Treat! What are you doing here?"

Closing her eyes, Cindy leaned against Travis briefly, knowing her legs would not support her just yet.

When she would have pulled free, Travis held on to her waist. "Don't go. Not yet. Did you hear the choir?"

Still off balance from the kiss, she shot him a confused look. "What?"

"The angelic choir. You must have heard it this time."

"I don't know what you're talking about. Let me

go, Travis." He dropped his hands, and she slid past him, running for the sanctuary of the kitchen.

"Well, well," Treat said. "Who was that? Did Mom come up with a third contender?"

Travis thought seriously about slugging his brother. He sure as hell wanted to hit something, and Treat always made an attractive target. She hadn't heard the music. It still reverberated in his ears. Taking a calming breath, Travis decided not to take his disappointment out on his brother. "No. I found this one all by myself. What are you doing here?"

"Mom called and asked me to fly down. I think she wants the loser in the competition for your hand to be able to make a quick getaway. She told me about the tests you dreamed up." Snickering, Treat raised his eyebrows in an exaggerated leer. "An essay? Sewing? That's the best you could do? Travis, old buddy, you need help."

"No, I don't. Not from you. What about business? Who's in charge? Or have you ruined us already?"

"Stuff it, Travis. You know your company runs like a well-oiled machine whether anyone's in charge or not."

"I am going to slug you." Travis advanced menacingly toward his brother. "And it's our company, not mine."

"Yeah, sure. You don't have to hit me—not over business. Dad's in charge. He got back from his fishing trip early. When I told him what was going on here, he decided he should spend a few days at the office." Treat picked up the suitcase he'd left sitting in the driveway after Manuel had dropped him off at the house. "Who is she?" he asked nonchalantly.

"Who?"

"The woman you were kissing."

"The housekeeper."

"Housekeeper? I don't think so. Come clean, bro. Where did you find her?"

"Right here. Mom hired her through an agency."

"Why were you kissing her?"

"Because." How could she not have heard the music this time? The damn—darn—angelic choir had been singing loud enough to shatter glass. Although, come to think of it, this time the singers had sounded more like a girl group from the sixties than a heavenly host of angels. Travis shoved his hands in his hair. He was losing it. Big-time.

Treat waved a hand in front of his face. "Hey. Pay attention. Tell me more about this housekeeper. Is she in the running for Great-Grandmother's engagement ring, too?"

"She won the race days ago, only she doesn't know it yet."

"Huh? I don't understand." Treat blinked once, then stared at him goggle-eyed. "Well, I'll be a son of a gun! You're in love with her!"

"Yeah. So?" If Treat dared to taunt him, he would hit him. Twice. First on his Roman nose. Next, on the cleft in his chin. Travis folded his fingers into fists, getting ready.

Treat clapped him on the shoulder. "That's great. You'll be married before you're thirty-five. You'll have kids in a year or two. Mom will be happy. Dad will be happy because Mom's happy. And me, I'll be happy because I'm off the hook."

"There's one little problem. Cindy doesn't love me."

"She sure doesn't hate you. That was some hot kiss I interrupted."

"She didn't hear the—" Travis stopped. He'd already said too much. Treat did not need to know about the heavenly music.

"Hear? What's hearing got to do with love?"

"You'll find out." Provided he wasn't the only man in the world who heard singing when he kissed the woman he loved.

"Have you told her how you feel?"

"Not exactly."

"Why not? How hard can it be? You say, 'I love you' and she says it back."

"What if she doesn't? I'm not ready for that."

Treat frowned, obviously having trouble with the notion that there was a woman in the world who could resist his older brother. "I guess that's possible. You aren't me. Okay. I can understand how you feel—no one likes to be rejected. But what's with the tests? Are you planning on settling for second-best?"

"No. I thought if I told Brooke and Stephanie I wanted them to write essays they'd turn tail and run. They didn't. Then Cindy started acting jealous, so I thought I'd let them hang around for a while."

"Fighting over you?"

Travis nodded. "Stupid idea. I'm going to tell them the whole thing is bogus, and you can take them both back to San Antonio."

"I don't know," Treat said. "From where I stood, it looked like your plan is working. The kiss was her idea, wasn't it?"

"Yeah." He ran his tongue over his lips, remembering her sweet taste. Treat was right. She had initiated the kiss. Cindy felt something for him. Maybe only attraction at this point, but attraction could blossom into love. In time.

The problem was there wasn't much time left. And if Brooke and Stephanie left, there might be even less time available. He had the feeling Cindy would be right behind them.

Glumly he followed Treat into the house. He could see it all now—Cindy wouldn't fall in love with him, and he would have two other women angry with him. Three, once his mother found out he'd found the right woman and let her get away. Travis groaned. "What a mess!"

"I would say I told you so, but I don't think I ever did."

"Told me what?"

"To avoid falling in love. As far as I can tell, it's almost always a mistake. Love makes a man do weird things. Like give up his freedom."

"Since when are you an expert? You've never been in love in your life."

"I am a shrewd observer of the human condition, especially as it relates to male-female interaction. Want the benefit of my long and arduous studies?"

"No. Yeah." Travis groaned again. He must really be desperate if he was asking his younger brother for advice.

"Tell the woman you love her. If she loves you, everything's rosy. If she doesn't, you may hurt for a while, but the sooner you find out, the sooner you'll get over it."

"I'll think about it." But, coward that he was, he knew he'd put that off for a little while longer. And there was always the chance that another test would do the trick. Seeing one more time how he inspired other women to compete fiercely for him, Cindy might finally realize what a prize he was. "Maybe later."

Treat gave him a pitying look. "Forget what I just said. You're right. I don't know diddly-squat about love. Let's go to Mexico and hit the bars. How about a tequila-drinking contest? A little lemon, a little salt, a lot of José Cuervo?"

"No. I've got to come up with a third contest."

"What for? You're not going to marry Brooke or Stephanie."

"I might. If Cindy doesn't love me, it won't matter who I marry." Travis sighed deeply. "Like you said, that would make three people happy—Mom, Dad and you. Four, if we assume my avaricious bride will also be filled with joy."

Treat snorted. "Cut the crap, bro. You're not built to be a martyr. And there's no real hurry. Nothing but tradition is pushing you toward a quick marriage. I say, stuff tradition. If you're sure she's your woman, go for it."

"I plan to. Now, about the third test—"

Treat snapped his fingers. "I know! A kissing contest. If you want to make her jealous, that ought to do the job."

"I don't want to kiss Brooke or Stephanie."

Treat gave him a look filled with awe. "No kidding? You must be in love. And trouble." He shuddered. "God, I hope that never happens to me."

Travis smiled grimly. "Love's not all fun and games, that's for damn sure. Cindy was right about that, too. She said marriage is serious."

"Too serious for me. Okay, if kissing is out, what

else can Cindy do better than Brooke and Stephanie?''

"She's a good cook.''

"That's cool. You can take turns in the kitchen.'' Treat shot him a quizzical look. "Unless you were smart enough to pretend you don't know your way around a skillet.''

"Nope. I fixed dinner one night.''

"Bad mistake. But I guess that's another consequence of being in love—no more secrets. Tell me again—what's so great about love?''

"The music, Treat. The music is heavenly.''

# 8

Cindy grabbed a dust cloth on her way through the kitchen and headed for the library. She'd hide out there until she regained her senses. And her equilibrium. Her knees still felt like rubber.

Why had she kissed Travis?

After stacking the albums and scrapbooks on one corner of the library table, she began polishing the table. Why did anyone kiss anyone? Lots of reasons. To say hello. Or goodbye. To thank someone. Some kisses punished, others aroused. One of those reasons, any of those reasons, she could accept. She had to. Otherwise she'd have to admit that...*no!*

She had not kissed Travis Rule because she loved him.

The library door opened.

"Cindy. My office. Now." Travis walked away, leaving the door open.

She had to go after him. He hadn't given her time to tell him she would not obey his curt order.

He was standing behind his desk when she entered his office. "Sit down."

"Travis, I—"

He handed her a stack of fax pages. "The leasing information, and the market survey."

Confused, she looked at the papers. "You called me in here for another lesson?"

He shoved one hand into his hair, jostling that cowlick free. "No. I want to tell you...something."

"That I'm fired?" Of course that was the reason. She'd stepped over the line. He could kiss her, but she, the housekeeper, could not return the favor and expect to stay employed. "I don't think that's fair." She stood up. "But I'll go."

"Please sit down, Cindy. I'm not going to fire you. I called you in here because..."

Whatever Travis was trying to tell her stuck in his throat for the second time. She sank back into the chair. "Because..."

"Because I wanted to tell you that I..." He took a deep breath. "Because I wanted to ask you if you would marry me." The words tumbled out of his mouth in a rush.

"What did you say?"

"I asked you if you would marry me. Please."

He leaned over the desk, and she caught a whiff of lemon and something else. "Travis Rule, have you been drinking?"

"No. Yes. One shot of tequila. Treat made me do it. He said I needed a little Cuervo courage. Well, will you?"

"Of course not." She stood up. "Will that be all?"

"Why not? Why won't you marry me? You kissed me."

"One kiss is no reason to get married."

"You kissed me more than once," he accused.

"So? That's still no reason to get married. And neither is your thirty-fifth birthday. That's what this is about, isn't it? Your family tradition?" Planting both hands on the edge of his desk, she glared at him. "Why are you asking me? Why not Brooke? Or Stephanie? Do you think I would be easier to control? Because I'd be grateful?"

He had that bewildered little-boy look again. "Grateful? Why should you be grateful? I'm the one who'd be grateful. If you marry me I won't have to spend the rest of my life alone. I don't want to be alone, Cindy."

"But why me? Brooke—"

"I don't want Brooke or Stephanie or any other woman. Mom—"

"Don't blame your mother for your problem! Why don't you act your age and tell your mother to stuff the family tradition?"

"This has nothing to do with family or tradition. You have to marry me, Cindy. I insist."

She sucked in her breath. "Insist all you want to. I wouldn't marry you if you were The Only Bachelor in Texas!" Cindy turned on her heel and walked out of the office, slamming the door behind her.

She didn't stop until she'd reached the sanctuary of her room. Closing the door behind her, she snapped the lock. Leaning against the door, shudders racking her body, she stared blindly at the opposite wall.

Travis Rule had proposed to her.

And a more insulting proposal she could not begin to imagine. In his office, holding faxes in his hand. No words of love. Not one.

Pushing away from the door, Cindy pulled the hairpins from her hair. She sat down at the dresser and began brushing her hair. "No wonder Travis has stayed a bachelor this long! No woman with a lick of sense would have him. He's bossy and conceited and…and…I love him so much." Her tirade ended on a sob.

Blinking back tears, Cindy stared at her reflection in the mirror. "Who said that? Not me. I don't love Travis."

The mirror reflected the truth shining in her eyes.

The truth was she'd loved him for months. She'd fallen in love the first time she'd seen his portrait over the fireplace in the family room. She'd fallen deeper in love every time she'd read his baby book and looked in the scrapbooks and photo albums.

And he wanted to marry her.

Only to meet a deadline, to fulfill a family tradition. Not because he loved her. She could never marry a man who did not love her.

And she couldn't stay at the Monarch Ranch and watch him propose to Brooke or Stephanie. Cindy picked up the telephone and dialed a New Orleans number.

"At Your Service."

"Fae Rae?"

"Yes. Cindy, is that you? How are you dear?"

"Fine," she whimpered. "A-awful."

"Oh, my. What's the matter? Are you sick? Hurt? Is anyone there? Are you all alone, Cindy?"

"I'm not alone. The Rules are here. Sal and Treat and T-Travis. And others. I can't stay here any longer, Fae Rae. You've got to find a replacement right away."

"Have they mistreated you in any way? I can't send a replacement if the Rules aren't good employers."

"No. They've been very kind. Generous. Friendly."

"Then I don't understand, Cindy, dear. Why do you want to leave?"

"Because I l-love him, and he doesn't love me," she wailed.

"Who doesn't love you?" Fae Rae sounded indignant.

"Travis. He k-kissed me, and he asked me to marry him, but he doesn't love me."

"Oh, my. Bennie was right again," whispered Fae Rae.

"Bennie? Your husband?" Cindy knew Fae Rae had been a widow for several years.

"Never you mind. Now, listen to me Cindy Ellerbee. I'll find a replacement, even if I have to come myself. But you stay put until I, or someone I send gets there. At Your Service does not leave clients in the lurch, and from what you've said, you've got a houseful to deal with."

"Oh, Fae Rae, I can't stay here. Not after he proposed. Not when he's going to keep on proposing until he finds a woman dumb enough to say yes."

"He's proposing to everyone?" Fae Rae sounded shocked.

"He hasn't yet. But I know he will. It's his family tradition, you see."

"He comes from a long line of Bluebeards? Don't answer that. I'd never get the signal about a bigamist."

"Signal? Fae Rae, you're not making any sense."

"Yes, I am. Do as I say, Cindy. Stay put. For only a little while longer. Promise me?" When Cindy didn't answer right away, she continued ruthlessly, "Remember that I believed in you when no one else did. You owe me this much."

Defeated, Cindy agreed. "I'll stay. But hurry, Fae Rae."

"I will. Don't worry, my dear. Everything will be all right."

Cindy hung up the telephone and reached for a tissue. Scrubbing the tears from her cheeks, she told herself she could do it. She could stay put. She could watch Travis make a fool of himself with his silly marriage tests and survive. It might even turn out to be good for her. Broken hearts built character.

If she kept this up, falling in love with the wrong man every year or so, by the time she reached thirty she might have more character than Mother Teresa, but her heart would look like a mosaic!

Muttering words that would have shocked the Hufstatler sisters out of a year's growth, Cindy twisted her hair back into a bun. "I refuse to wallow in misery! There is no reason to be miserable—I'm not going to die of love. I'll survive this!"

She still had her needlework shop to look forward to. But she wouldn't open shop in San Antonio. That left plenty of other places. Dallas, Houston, Fort Worth. Not that she had to stay in Texas. She could go anywhere. She had no ties, no family and, except for Fae Rae, no friends.

With a sigh and a sniffle, Cindy pushed away from the dresser and walked to the bed. She lay down, burying her face in the pillow. Maybe she would wallow in misery. Just for an hour or two. Within minutes she was asleep.

Travis sat at his desk, numb. He couldn't feel, and he couldn't think straight. Nothing new there. He hadn't had a sensible thought since Cindy had tumbled off the library ladder into his arms. He never would have followed Treat's advice if he'd been thinking.

The door opened, and his advisor strolled into his office.

"You!"

"Yeah. Me. Were you expecting someone else? Cindy? Are you going to tell her you—"

"She's been here already. I did what you said. I asked her to marry me." Travis snarled the words.

Treat sat down on the edge of the desk and looked at him. "Let me guess. She said no."

"Emphatically." Travis stood up. "This is your fault. I'm going to have to hit you."

Treat backed away from the desk, raising his fists. "My fault? How do you figure that?"

"The tequila. The advice—tell her you love her, you said. Ask her to marry you." Travis balled his fist and aimed for Treat's chin.

Treat blocked the blow with his forearm. "You never followed my advice before."

"I shouldn't have done it this time. I knew it was too soon. I felt it in my gut." He swung again, this time connecting. Treat's head snapped back.

"Feel this, too." Treat hit him in the stomach, bending him over.

The office door opened again. "Boys! I thought I heard something. Stop fighting this instant. What on earth has gotten into you two? You haven't brawled like this in years." Sal stood in the doorway, hands on hips. "Travis, straighten up. Brooke and Stephanie are waiting for you in the family room. They've finished mending."

"You know what?" Travis gasped. "I don't give a damn."

Tapping her foot, Sal glared at him. "Think again, son. I raised you to be a gentleman, and gentlemen treat their guests politely. Get in there!" She pointed in the direction of the family room.

"I'm going." Rubbing his stomach, Travis headed out the door.

"Me, too," said Treat, sidling by his mother.

"You'd better go to the kitchen first and have Cindy put a piece of steak on that eye.

"Good idea," Treat said, winking at Travis with his good eye. "Cindy may need a little company about now."

Grinding his teeth together, Travis joined Brooke and Stephanie. He nodded a curt greeting and headed for the bar.

"There you are. What took you so long?" asked Brooke. "I'm dying for a margarita."

"Me, too," said Stephanie. "Then you can tell us what the next test will be."

Taking a pitcher of frozen margaritas from the tiny refrigerator under the counter, he said, "There won't be a next test," said Travis. Cindy's refusal had settled his fate, as far as he was concerned. He'd be a bachelor for the rest of his life. "Another test isn't necessary."

"Of course it is, silly man. The score is tied. I won the first test, and Brooke won the second. Her grandmother taught her to darn, darn it," said Stephanie, a coy smile on her face. "One more test. And soon."

"Soon." Travis nodded, distracted by the thought of what Treat and Cindy might be up to in the kitchen. When Treat had headed in that direction, he'd had that look in his eye, the acquisitive gleam he got whenever he tried to take something away from his older brother.

"Whatever it is, let's do it tomorrow," said Brooke. "This has gone on long enough."

"Tomorrow. Right," agreed Travis. Cindy might be packing her bags, even now, he thought, panicking. Why had he jumped the gun? He'd known it was too soon to tell her how he felt. Handing a frosty, salt-rimmed glass to Brooke, he frowned. He had told Cindy how he felt, hadn't he?

"Thanks. Well, are you going to tell us, or not?" asked Brooke, taking a sip of the margarita.

"Tell you what?" he asked, paying attention to his guests for the first time since he'd entered the room.

"What the next test is?" Stephanie picked up her drink. "You said you'd let us know tonight."

"I did?" He was losing what was left of his mind. He couldn't remember one thing he'd said since Cindy had turned down his offer of marriage.

"Yes, you did. Well?" asked Stephanie, arching one elegant blond brow.

"I don't know." Where was Treat? Where was Cindy? "I need to check on something," he said.

"Not yet," Stephanie said, clutching his arm with a surprisingly strong grip.

He wouldn't get away from them until he came up with a third test. And he might as well continue with the melodrama he'd concocted, even if the plot had taken twists he hadn't anticipated. Once the tests were over, and he'd refused to marry either the winner or the loser, Brooke and Stephanie would spread the word. Not only was Travis Rule crazy, he was a liar to boot. That should end his eligibility, once and for all.

Taking Stephanie's hand off his arm, he said, "Cooking. Each of you will plan a meal and cook it. Tomorrow."

"Plan a meal?" Stephanie flashed a confident smile. "That's almost too easy. I've planned many dinner parties in my time. For as many as two hundred. How many will be at this meal?"

"Two. Me and the cook."

"How romantic," sighed Stephanie.

"You keep saying *cook*," said Brooke. "Surely you don't expect your wife to cook after you're married. What are servants for?"

"I want a wife who knows how to cook. You never know what the future holds. Businesses fail every day."

"What have you heard?" asked Stephanie, blanching. "I mean—Monarch's not in trouble, is it?"

"No."

Visibly relieved, Stephanie nodded. "All right. Which meal?"

"Draw straws." He reached for a cocktail pick. Snapping it in two, he tucked the pieces into his fist. "Short straw gets lunch, long gets dinner."

"We can't both do dinner?" asked Stephanie.

"No." He held out his hand, and they both took a straw.

Brooke held up the short half of the cocktail pick. "Lunch for me," she announced. "I think a picnic would be nice. Is there a private place we could go?"

"Yeah. I know just the place."

"That leaves dinner for me," said Stephanie. "A

romantic dinner for two, tomorrow night.'' She stood up. ''I'll work up a menu.''

Both women headed for the kitchen, leaving Travis behind, contemplating his sins.

Cindy handed Treat the ice bag just as Stephanie and Brooke entered the kitchen.

''What happened to you?'' asked Stephanie, heading for the pantry, a pad and pencil in hand.

''I ran into my brother's fist,'' said Treat, holding the ice bag to his eye. ''What's up?''

Stephanie stepped out of the pantry. ''We're cooking for Travis tomorrow,'' she said. ''That's the final test—cooking a romantic meal for two. We drew for the meal, and I won dinner. Lucky for me I took a cooking course the last time I was in Paris. I'm making a list of the things I'll need.''

''Cooking, huh? That's interesting. I have to say, I don't understand the reasoning behind these tests Travis has come up with,'' Treat said, smiling at Cindy.

Cindy ignored him and concentrated on Stephanie.

''I, for one, think cooking is a brilliant idea,'' Stephanie said. ''Food can be a metaphor for...other appetites, don't you think?'' She didn't wait for an answer. ''The mouth-watering anticipation, fueled by scents of exotic spices. That first nibble of an appetizer, a teasing taste to prepare the senses for what will follow. Then the main course, bite after delicious bite of satisfying, sensual foods. Finally, dessert, something sweet and sinful to tantalize the tongue. Not so much to mark the end of the meal, more of a prelude to what will...may follow. Oh, my. Listen to me ramble on.'' She lowered her head, but not before

Cindy saw the triumphant gleam in Stephanie's cat green eyes.

Cindy, feeling more than a little catlike herself, wanted to scratch the glitter right out of Stephanie's eyes. Instead, she asked, "How about you, Brooke? What are you planning?"

Sighing, Brooke said. "I drew lunch. I'm taking Travis on a picnic."

"And what will you feed Travis, Brooke, dear? Peanut butter sandwiches and potato chips?" Stephanie asked, a nasty grin marring her bow-shaped lips.

"Exactly. How did you guess?" asked Brooke.

"I knew you couldn't cook." Stephanie smiled, a confident glitter shining in her eyes. "Treat, darling, would you drive me to the nearest grocery store this afternoon? I've got my menu all worked out, and I need a few things." Taking Treat by the arm, she led him from the kitchen.

"Bitch," muttered Brooke, slamming the cookbook shut. "She's going to win."

"Looks that way," said Cindy, trying hard not to care. Travis had insulted her and Brooke—and even Stephanie—with his clumsy quest for a bride. Still, she couldn't help wishing he would come to his senses and wait for a woman he could love. "Are you giving up?"

"I should. I can't boil water." Brooke leaned back in the chair. "Not that it really matters. I don't want to marry Travis. But, darn it, I *hate* losing. Especially to her." Brooke grinned at her. "What the heck. He may like peanut butter and jelly sandwiches."

Treat stuck his head through the back door. "Cindy, why don't you come with us? You can practice driving on the highway. Brooke, do you need anything?''

''Yeah. A gourmet takeout place.''

''Huh?''

''Never mind. Go with him, Cindy. If you stay, I might try to talk you into showing me how to fry chicken and make potato salad.''

Cindy reluctantly followed Treat out the door and through the breezeway to the garage. She didn't want to go to Carrizo with Treat and Stephanie. They both asked too many questions.

Stephanie was waiting by the car, tapping her foot impatiently. Treat opened the rear door for her. ''You don't mind the back seat do you, Steph? Cindy will be driving, and I need to sit in the copilot's seat.''

''Whatever,'' said Stephanie.

Once she was behind the wheel, Cindy turned to Treat. ''I don't know about this. Are you sure I'm ready for the highway?''

''We won't know until you try. But don't worry. There's not much traffic, not even in town. You can handle it.''

Cindy started the car and backed out of the drive. Most of the trip into town was accomplished in silence, except for Treat's helpful instructions, which she had no difficulty in following. Being confined in a small space with him did not make her heart beat faster or her breathing shallow. She could concentrate on driving. She'd almost relaxed when she caught a glimpse of Stephanie in the back seat.

Stephanie's eyes narrowed, and her eyebrows pulled together in a frown. ''Aren't you a little old for driving lessons?'' she asked.

Turning her attention back to the road, Cindy answered, "I have my driver's license. I know how to drive an automatic."

"I should think you would. What kind of house-keeper can't drive herself to the grocery store? Where did you work before Travis found you?"

"New Orleans."

"New Orleans? Really? I went to Newcomb College for a few semesters. I adore New Orleans. Who did you work for? I may know them."

"Michael and Mercedes Freret," she said, unable to think of a reason not to reveal her former employers' names. Still, she had an uneasy feeling. What if Stephanie knew the Frerets?

"Hmm. I've heard of them. He owns lots of car dealerships, doesn't he? I don't think we've ever met, however. I'll have to ask Caro about them the next time I talk to her. Caroline Hebert was my college roommate and she's a native New Orleanian. Were you their housekeeper or the cook?"

Stephanie hadn't heard of the scandal surrounding her departure from the Freret household. Cindy breathed a sigh of relief. She had enough to deal with for the next few days without having old wounds re-opened. Especially with someone like Stephanie around, ready and willing to pour salt. "Neither. I looked after their children."

"You were a nanny?" Stephanie's tone was disbelieving. "I never would have thought—I mean, you and children?"

"I'm sure Cindy is very good with kids," said Treat, frowning. "What did you think, Steph? That she'd cook them like Hansel and Gretel?"

"Of course not," said Stephanie. "One wonders why she would leave the children behind, though."

"They grew up. They didn't need me any longer."

"I see. But still, what *could* be the attraction for your present position? Other than money, I mean. I'm sure Travis is a very generous employer. But you're so isolated way out here. So alone." She paused. "Or perhaps not. Perhaps you enjoy company from time to time?"

Choosing to evade Stephanie's suggestive questions, Cindy said, "I like being alone." Cindy was afraid that might not be strictly true anymore, but she'd had enough of Stephanie's grilling. "Could we please not talk? I've never driven a stick shift on the highway before, and I need to pay attention."

"You certainly do. The last thing I need is to be involved in an accident. I can't miss dinner tomorrow night. That reminds me. Treat, be a dear and take everyone out to dinner tomorrow, will you? I want to be alone with Travis."

"No problem. But you won't be alone unless Cindy comes along, too."

"She can't go. I need her to serve the meal."

"I thought you were supposed to do this on your own," said Treat.

"I will plan and cook it all by myself. But Travis won't expect me to serve it. I am *not* a servant."

# 9

The next day came too soon. The days were rushing by too quickly, Cindy thought, although she couldn't explain why time suddenly seemed too short. Too short for what? She couldn't wait for Fae Rae to send a replacement. She wanted the time to fly, so that she could leave Monarch Ranch and Travis Rule behind her and get on with her life.

She paced her room, waiting for Brooke and Travis to return from their picnic. Her chores were done. The beds were made, the dishes washed, and she had no meals to prepare for the rest of the day.

As soon as Cindy had cleaned up after Brooke's cooking, Stephanie had taken over the kitchen. Sal was in her room reading. Treat had left early that morning, joining the three cowboys in moving cattle from one area of the ranch to another. She had no one to talk to and nothing to do to take her mind off the minutes speedily ticking away.

Sitting down at the tiny desk in the corner of her room, Cindy took a notebook out of the drawer. She'd go over the plan for her needlework shop. Perhaps if she reviewed her notes, she would be able to recapture the excitement she'd felt while dreaming about her new, independent life. Staring at the pages of the notebook, she forced herself to read, concentrating so fiercely that she managed to block out all thought of Travis and Brooke.

The clatter of a cowbell interrupted her. With a groan, Cindy rose from her desk. Very slowly. Facing Stephanie in her present state of mind was the last thing she wanted to do. She needed more time to get used to the idea of being in unrequited love.

The bell clattered again. With a sigh, Cindy reached for her apron and headed for the kitchen.

Stephanie was putting decorative bits of pastry on the top crust of an apple pie. "There you are. Clean up this mess, will you? I still have to prepare the sauce for the chateaubriand, and this clutter is in my way. What do you think of my menu? Elegant, but elemental. Travis is a typical Texas male—a steak-and-potatoes man. Voilà! I will feed him chateau-briand and potatoes Anna."

"I'll get right on it, as soon as I—"

"Now. I want to get everything except the last-minute touches completed. I need a few hours before dinner to prepare myself for tonight. Have you seen Travis?"

"Today?"

"Stupid. Of course today. Brooke came in a few minutes ago, looking entirely too happy. The picnic must have been a success."

"That's nice," said Cindy. Picturing Brooke and Travis on a blanket under the cottonwood trees almost brought on another mournful sigh. She swallowed hard and managed to hold it in. Briskly she began placing mixing bowls and measuring cups in the dish-washer.

Wielding a wire whisk, Stephanie frowned at her.

"Nice? I don't think so. You didn't help her, did you?"

"No. She made the peanut butter and jelly sandwiches all by herself."

"Don't get snotty with me. I'm going to win this contest. If you want to stay on here, you'd better behave yourself."

"Yes, Miss Lord," said Cindy. She didn't care what Stephanie thought about her, but she shouldn't do anything to lose the Monarch Ranch account for At Your Service.

"That's better. The picnic can't have been much of a success then, with only sandwiches. Unless Brooke did something to take Travis's mind off food," muttered Stephanie. "Are you sure you haven't seen him?"

"Not since he and Brooke left. Maybe he went to help Treat and the others with the cattle." Cindy finished wiping off the kitchen counters. "Is there anything else you'd like me to do?"

"Not right now, but I have instructions for you about this evening. Dinner will begin promptly at seven. That's unfashionably early, I know, but Treat has promised to vacate the premises no later than six-thirty. I want to have plenty of time for dinner and...things, before the others return."

What *things?* Cindy wanted to ask. Except she didn't have to—it was obvious Stephanie planned to seduce Travis, right in front of her. "What about me?" She couldn't keep the indignation out of her voice.

"What about you? You'll be here, in uniform, to serve us. Set the table now, and get that out of the way. Place us side by side, not at opposite ends of the table. I want to be close to Travis during the meal. There are four courses—soup, entree, salad and dessert, in that order, à la française. We'll have wine— I found a decent burgundy at the liquor store—with the chateaubriand, and champagne with the apple tart.'' Stephanie frowned. ''A chocolate soufflé would be more impressive, but I'd have to leave the table to finish preparing it.'' She nodded to herself. ''Apple pie is a good choice. Makes a man think of hearth and home, don't you agree?''

''I suppose so,'' said Cindy.

''And there will be whipped cream to top it. As soon as you've poured the champagne, make yourself scarce. I'll take care of serving the cream.'' She licked her lips suggestively.

''I'll just bet you will,'' muttered Cindy.

''What was that?''

''Nothing. I'll get the crystal and china.''

''Don't forget to polish the silver. I want everything to be perfect tonight.''

And so it was, as far as Cindy could tell. Perfect for Stephanie. And for Travis. Stephanie had dressed in a frothy silk chiffon creation that showcased her lush bosom and tiny waist. The dress was black, of course. What other color would a seductress wear? Diamonds sparkled at her ears, and another, which hung from a thin gold chain, glittered in the shadow between her breasts.

Travis had dressed with equal care, in a dark suit and white shirt. Cindy sniffed. He must have figured out that he was the main course on Stephanie's menu. Why did he have to look so handsome and appealing? And, if that weren't enough, why did he have to be a man who honored his mother's wishes, who took care of his family, who shared his business knowledge?

Watching another woman tempt and tantalize the man she loved was almost more than she could bear. She should never have agreed to this…torture. She'd had other choices. She could have gone to Mexico with Treat, Brooke and Sal. Dolores and Manuel would have been pleased to see her if she'd decided to pay them a visit. Gus would have welcomed her at the bunkhouse for another cooking lesson.

But no, she'd stayed. Love must make a person masochistic.

With each course, Cindy's composure slipped another notch. During the soup course, Stephanie whispered in Travis's ear, her voice husky and so low that Cindy could only guess what she was saying. Whatever it was seemed to have Travis transfixed.

When the steak was served, Stephanie fed bites to Travis, dipping each morsel in her perfect béarnaise sauce, wiping tiny drips from his mouth and chin with her fingers. That went on much too long, long enough that Cindy had time to fantasize another culinary disaster to befall Stephanie. She'd already wished, futilely as it turned out, for the cream soup to curdle and the steak to burn. A wilted salad was too mild.

Food poisoning! Perfect! That would punish both of them for putting her through this torture. She would enjoy seeing both of them on the floor, writhing in agony.

But nothing bad happened.

The soup had stayed smooth and creamy, the steak had turned out exactly right, and they both appeared in good health. Any writhing that took place that night would not be in agony. The thought of Travis making love to Stephanie made Cindy's stomach churn. Miss Hufstatler would have said, "God's punishment, Cindy! Wish food poisoning on others, and it's you who'll be sick."

Retreating to the kitchen after removing the salad plates, Cindy arranged two dessert plates, the apple pie and a bowl of whipped cream on a tray. Stephanie had specified that she herself would slice the pie and serve the cream.

Pushing the dining room door open with her hip, Cindy entered the dining room. Stephanie had moved her chair even closer to Travis. She was practically in his lap.

"Ellerbee. Don't just stand there. Put the tray down and leave us." Softening her voice to a sexy purr, she added, "Travis, darling, why don't you open the champagne while I slice the pie?"

Cindy placed the pie and the silver serving knife in front of Stephanie as Travis popped the cork on the champagne bottle. He filled Stephanie's crystal flute and then his own. Setting the bottle down, he raised his glass. "To us," he said, looking straight into Cindy's eyes.

"To us," echoed Stephanie, touching her glass to his. She took a sip, then set her glass on the table. Reaching for the bowl of cream, she gave Travis a sultry smile. "Whipped cream?"

Travis nodded.

"Where would you like it? On the pie, or...on me?"

That did it. Cindy took the champagne bottle and upended it over their heads. With Travis's startled gasp and Stephanie's outraged shriek echoing in her ears, she fled.

Cindy made it to her room before Travis caught up with her. Her pulse ratcheted up another notch when he locked the door behind him. Champagne dripping from his eyebrows and chin, Travis advanced toward her, step by inexorable step. When he had her backed against the wall, he stopped and asked softly, "Why did you do that, Cindy?"

Travis had a gleam in his eyes she didn't recognize. Anger? Disgust? "I—I don't know." She'd acted without thinking. She still couldn't think clearly, not with her heart pounding loudly in her ears, not with Travis standing so close.

"Don't you? It wasn't very nice. Stephanie is very upset."

More than upset. Cindy could hear her, yelling swearwords at the top of her lungs. Clearing her throat, Cindy nodded. "I can tell. Are you...upset?"

"You could say that, but then, in one way or another I've been 'upset' for days. I'm curious, too. Why would you feel the need to pour champagne on my head?"

"Because you...she...whipped cream," babbled Cindy, trying to push herself through the wall.

He leaned toward her and whispered conspiratorially, "Are you saying you didn't want me licking whipped cream off Stephanie's—"

"Travis!"

"Could it be that you're jealous?" He reached out and casually plucked a hairpin from her hair.

Tucking the strand of hair freed by him back into her bun, Cindy aimed her nose at the ceiling. "Jealous? Me? Certainly not."

"Are you sure about that?" He moved closer, so close she could see the flecks of gold flashing in his blue eyes. He removed two more hairpins, and her hair fell around her shoulders. "There, that's better. Now, about Stephanie—"

"I am not jealous!" she lied. She would not give him the satisfaction of knowing how thoroughly the green monster had her in its grip. "If you must know, I poured champagne on you because...because you were behaving inappropriately. Both of you."

Rubbing his dripping chin thoughtfully, he nodded. "Right. Inappropriate behavior. That's a real good reason for a champagne shower. You're sure you aren't jealous?"

"Positive!"

"Because you have no reason to be. I don't give a rat's ass about Stephanie."

Cindy stared at him. "You don't?"

"Nope. She's not a very nice woman. She treats you like a servant."

"I *am* a servant."

"Not hers. Mine." He backed off a step or two, and she let out the breath she'd been holding. "I need a little service now, Cindy."

"Service?" she repeated blankly.

"This champagne is awfully sticky." He shrugged out of his suit coat. "And it's getting stickier by the minute." He untied his tie and stripped it off. Then he began unbuttoning his shirt.

"W-what are you doing?" she asked, staring at the triangle of bare chest right under her nose.

"Getting out of these wet clothes. I need a bath. And you're going to give me one."

"I am n-not," she said. Her voice sounded weak and shaky, almost as weak and shaky as her knees had gone at the thought of bathing Travis. Cindy cleared her throat and tried again. "I'm not giving you a bath. That's not in my job description."

Travis put one hand on the wall next to her head. "I don't remember that pouring champagne over me and Steph was of your duties, either." He put his mouth next to her ear and growled, "Get a wet washcloth. Now."

Cindy scooted sideways along the wall, then backed into the bathroom. When her backside bumped into the sink, she turned around and reached for a washcloth. Wetting it under the running faucet, she took deep, steadying breaths. She would wash off the champagne, only because she felt a teeny bit guilty about dousing him with it, not because he ordered her to in that bossy way he had.

He didn't scare her.

Returning to the bedroom, she found Travis barechested and reaching for his belt buckle. "There's no reason to take off your pants!" she gasped.

His hand stilled. "I guess you're right. Most of the champagne landed on my head and shoulders. Well, what are you waiting for? Wash me off."

The loud clatter of a cowbell ringing sounded. "That's Stephanie. She probably needs me—"

"I *need* you more. And I got to you first. Come here, Cindy."

"W-what for?"

"You know what for. I'm sticky and wet, a real mess. Your mess, Cindy. You made it. Clean it up."

She thought briefly about tossing the dripping cloth to him and telling him to clean himself up. She might have poured the champagne, but he'd started it, with his insulting proposal and his silly tests. But he didn't look like he was in the mood for an argument, and maybe, just maybe, she was a little bit afraid—not of him. Only of the way he made her feel.

Cindy moved closer. Standing on tiptoe, she quickly ran the wet cloth over his head and face. "There. All done." She backed out of reach.

"My chest is still sticky. And my shoulders."

With a shuddering sigh, she moved closer and began washing his broad shoulders and hard, bronzed chest. Her breathing became ragged, and her pulse raced faster with every touch.

So did his. He snagged her wrist and took the wet washcloth away. Tossing it to the floor, he wrapped both arms around her waist and pulled her closer.

"W-what are you doing?"

"Time for a little experiment."

She maneuvered her hands between them and pushed. Ineffectually. Travis didn't budge. "Oh, no. You're not testing me. I'm not after the prize."

"No? I think you are. And, one way or another, I'm going to prove it." If she didn't know better, she'd have thought he sounded desperate.

"How?" she scoffed, trying to wiggle free. "I've already turned down your offer of marriage." She knew what he was up to now. Humiliation. Hers. To even the score for what she'd done to his romantic dinner for two.

"Yeah, well this experiment isn't about marriage, Cindy. This is how it's going to go. First, I'm going to kiss you. Again and again, until you can't stand up. If that doesn't do it, I'm going to strip you naked and make love to you until you hear the damn music and admit you love me."

Aha! She was right. Travis wanted her to confess

she loved him so he could gloat— ''Music? What music?''

''The choir. Or the girl group. Either way, it will mean you love me as much as I love you.''

She stopped wiggling. ''You love me?''

''From the first day I saw you. You fell into my arms, and I heard angels singing.''

''Angels?''

''Maybe not. It could have been the Supremes.''

''What were they singing?''

''Hallelujah! Shut up, and I'll show you. Maybe this time when I kiss you, you'll finally hear them.''

He looked determined and something else. Anxious. Could it be he really didn't know she loved him? She supposed it could. She hadn't known until a heartbeat ago how he felt about her.

Travis Rule loved her!

That changed everything. Angling her head to one side, Cindy gave him a saucy grin. Travis was being awfully bossy. And, anxious or not, he was still trying to intimidate her. He deserved to suffer, a little. Before he could see the joy and love shining from her eyes, she closed them tightly. Wrapping her arms around his neck, she pressed against his wet chest and tilted her chin up. ''Kiss away, Travis. I can handle your experiment.''

His mouth touched hers gently, coaxing her lips to soften and part. Taking immediate advantage as soon as she opened her mouth, he plunged his tongue inside.

Oh, wow! Strike up the band!

Cindy kept her eyes squeezed shut. He wasn't going to get his way that easily. She could hold out for one or two more kisses before she told him what he wanted to hear. What else had he threatened? Something about stripping her naked and making love. That could work.

Cindy heard pounding. Loud pounding. Her heart? Or his?

"Travis Rule! Are you in there with her! Let me in!"

Dragging his mouth from hers, Travis shouted, "Go away, Stephanie. I'm busy." He looked at Cindy. "Where were we? Oh, yeah, I remember." His gaze slid from her mouth to her body. "You're all wet. How did that happen?"

"The washcloth…your chest was wet when you—"

"Did you hear the music?"

"No. But—"

He twirled her around and unzipped her dress. "Time for Plan B."

"Travis, this isn't necessary. I—"

"Yes, it is. I'm not letting you out of this room until you admit you love me." He pulled the dress from her shoulders and turned her back around. "That's better. I hate those nanny dresses."

Reflexes had Cindy crossing her arms over her still-decently covered body—she always wore a full slip under her uniforms. "I do love you, Travis. I fell in love with you before I ever met you. Maybe that's why I don't hear the music. I don't need music to tell me how much I love you."

He picked her up by the waist, lifting her until she was at eye level with him. He grinned at her. A cocky, conceited grin. "It was the baby book, wasn't it?"

"Probably. Although, to be completely honest,

Treat was a prettier baby.'' She put her hands on his shoulders. ''Put me down, Travis.''

''Not yet. So you think Treat is better looking, do you? Maybe I'd better proceed with Plan B after all. I wouldn't want you to be susceptible to his charms.''

She wiggled experimentally, trying to touch the floor with her toes. Travis didn't seem to notice. ''You think I won't be susceptible to him after you make love to me?''

Hugging her close, Travis backed toward the bed. ''Damn straight.'' He fell backward onto the bed, hauling her down on top of him. Nibbling on her neck, he muttered, ''Then you'll know for certain that you're my woman.''

Cindy slid off his chest and landed on her side, next to him. Propping her head on one hand, she drew her brows together in a mock frown. ''Your woman? That's a rather primitive concept, isn't it?''

He rolled onto his side, facing her. Brushing a lock of her hair out of her eyes, he smiled. ''Downright cave mannish. But it works both ways. I'm your man. You can count on me, Cindy. I plan to love you forever.''

''Me, too.'' She wound her arms around his neck and pulled that tempting mouth close to hers. ''I love you so much.''

That earned her another kiss. A slow, gentle kiss, full of passion and promises. When it ended, Travis looked deeply into her eyes. He had a look she recognized. Cocky. ''Now that you've admitted how you feel, I guess I won't have to strip you naked and make love to you, after all.''

''Did I say I loved you?'' She frowned. ''I don't

think so. You must have misunderstood. Perhaps you'd better proceed with Plan B, after all.''

Travis laughed. ''You're a tease, Cindy Ellerbee.''

''Who's teasing?'' She pushed him onto his back and sprawled on top of him.

''Cindy, are you sure—''

She stopped him with a kiss. With her lips still touching his, she sighed, ''I've never been surer of anything in my life, Travis. Strip me naked and make love to me.''

''You got it, sweetheart.'' Travis sat up with her in his arms. Sliding the straps of her slip off her shoulders, he pushed the garment to her waist. ''Lift your hips,'' he whispered, nuzzling her neck.

Cindy helped him maneuver the slip past her hips and off, revealing her white cotton bra and panties to his gaze.

''Such prim-and-proper underwear, Ms. Ellerbee.'' Travis grinned at her as he reached behind her back to unhook her bra.

''I'm a prim-and-proper sort of woman.'' Cindy shrugged out of the bra. ''Except with you. This isn't the first time you've seen me naked, remember?''

''I'll never forget having you naked on this bed, Cindy.'' He bent her back over his arm and gazed at her breasts. ''But I've never seen this view. You're beautiful.''

''I want to see you, too.'' Cindy twisted in his arms and reached for his belt buckle. Seconds later they were both naked. Travis leaned back against the headboard of the bed, and Cindy knelt beside him, staring. ''Wow,'' she said softly.

''Wow? Does that mean I'll do?''

''Oh, definitely. Is it all right to touch?''

"Touching is required. Start anywhere."

With trembling fingers, Cindy stroked Travis's shoulder. His skin was warm and silky. Pressing harder, she discovered the steel beneath the silk. "You're hard," she noted, skimming her hand from his shoulder to his chest.

"I'm getting there," Travis groaned.

Cindy shifted her position, moving to kneel between his thighs. Now she could use both hands to explore, to caress, to arouse. "Yes, you are, aren't you?"

Travis began his own exploration, sliding his hands from her shoulders to her waist to her thighs, then back up her abdomen to rest beneath her breasts. "Don't stop there," Cindy ordered, leaning forward.

"Is this what you want?" Travis took her breasts in his hands.

Her back arching, Cindy moaned, "Oh, yes." Her nipples became tight little pleasure buds, sending heat and desire flooding through her.

Travis moved one leg between hers, and she immediately reacted by squeezing his muscled thigh between hers. "Oh, that feels...so...good." Throwing her head back she rode his thigh, while his hands still fondled her aching breasts.

Pulling her astride his waist, Travis took one nipple into his mouth and sucked hard. Cindy screamed.

Travis laughed, his mouth still fastened on her breast, muffling the sound. "Shh," gasped Cindy. "Someone will hear you."

Raising his head, Travis smiled at her. "Me? I'm not the one who screamed like a banshee."

"You laughed at me."

"I laughed because I made you scream. I like making you scream. I think I'll do it again." He flipped her over on her back, coming down on top of her.

"I'm not too heavy am I?" he asked, taking her hands in his and holding them above her head.

"No. I can't...breathe, but that doesn't...seem to matter," she sighed, kissing the side of his neck.

Releasing her hands, Travis shifted some of his weight to his elbows. "Better?" When she nodded, he kissed her mouth, plunging his tongue into the sweet heat behind her parted lips again and again.

When she was clinging helplessly to him, Travis moved between her legs. With one stroke, he entered her.

Cindy screamed again, but this time her mouth was on his, and he swallowed her cry. He kept still. "I hurt you. Cindy, I'm so sorry."

"No. I'm not hurt." She wiggled experimentally. "I feel full, almost too full. It's a good feeling."

"It gets better." Travis began moving, withdrawing, then reentering her tight passage, slowly at first, until she began moving with him. Then faster and faster, until pleasure exploded between them, and Cindy cried out once more.

When she'd recovered enough to be aware of her surroundings, Cindy opened her eyes. Travis was on his side next to her, one arm bent to support his head, the other wrapped possessively around her waist. "Well?" he asked, a smug grin on his face.

"Well, what?" she asked.

"How do you feel?"

"Fine."

"Fine? That's all?" He looked disappointed. Dismayed, actually. Did she really make him unsure of himself?

"Fantastic?"

"That's better. I can live with fantastic." He sat up. "We'd better get dressed. Mom and the others will be back soon, and we have an announcement to make."

"Announcement?" It was her turn to be dismayed. "Your going to *announce* what we just did? To your mother?" Scandalized, Cindy felt her cheeks grow hot.

Pulling her into his arms, Travis laughed out loud. "No, sweetheart. Our engagement. I'm going to announce our engagement. We're getting married."

"You sure are bossy." She got off the bed, wiggling enough so that he'd be sorry he let her go, and headed for her closet.

"Complaining already?"

"Just a little. What do you suppose Stephanie is up to? I haven't heard the cowbell for a while."

"Maybe she flew away on her broom."

Cindy swallowed a giggle. "You did mislead her."

"Yeah, I did. But she'll get over it."

"Brooke, too. What about her? She's not like Stephanie. She's nice."

"True, but she was never a contender. For two reasons. One, she's not you. And two, she's in love with someone else."

"She told you about Joe? When?"

"At the picnic. She had to do something to fill the time after I told her I hate peanut butter."

"Poor Brooke."

"She wishes. She'd like to be poor. Then that guy she's in love with would marry her. I told her if she wanted to be poor, go for it. Just because she inherited a fortune doesn't mean she has to keep it. So she's going to set up a philanthropic foundation.''

"Brooke is going to give her money away?"

"Every penny. Said she'd go to what's-his-name with the clothes on her back and—"

"And what?"

"She hoped they wouldn't stay on her back too long.''

It was Cindy's turn to blush. "Oh. My. But, Travis, what a wonderful idea you had! She'll get the man she loves, and she'll help hundreds of other people at the same time.''

"Yeah, I'm brilliant. You're very lucky to get me."

She snorted. "I suppose so. But I still don't understand. Why did you go through with the testing? If you fell in love with me at first sight?"

"I didn't know how you felt about me. How could I? One minute you were hitting me with a spoon, and the next minute you were kissing me. You thought I was spoiled and conceited. And you said no when I proposed.''

"Only because you didn't tell me you loved me. And you *are* conceited. With some reason, I have to admit. I tried concentrating on your faults so I could stay away from you. One touch of your tempting mouth, and I would have been a goner. I knew that.''

"Oh-ho. So you think my mouth is tempting, do you?"

"I should never have told you that. Now you'll be able to get your way anytime you want to, just with a kiss.''

"What power! I feel like I could conquer the world.''

"I thought you'd already done that—you are The Richest Bachelor in Texas."

"Not for much longer. We're going to have a very short engagement, followed by a very long marriage with lots of babies."

"Oh, T-Travis. Babies. I'm going to have a f-family of my very own." Her eyes misted over.

Travis took her in his arms. "Don't cry, Cindy. You've already got a family. Mom loves you and so will Dad, as soon as he meets you. Treat thinks you're dangerous, but he'll learn to love you, too."

"Dangerous?" she sniffled. "Me? Why?"

"You stole my heart, my precious thief."

"Thief? Travis, there's something I have to tell you. About Etienne and—"

"Not now." He let her go and walked to the door, picking up his shirt and jacket on the way. "Get dressed and meet me in Mom's room."

"Travis, wait." The door shut, and she was alone.

# 10

Hugging herself, Cindy flopped back on the bed and stared dreamily at the ceiling. She was loved! Thousands of remembered dreams kaleidoscoped through her brain. Travis would be her husband. She wouldn't have to pretend she liked being alone ever again. She would be a wife, a mother, just as she'd always wanted. With a tremulous sigh, Cindy let her eyes flutter shut, then opened them wide.

Travis wanted her to meet him in the master suite. Cindy jumped up and dressed quickly in jeans and a pink cotton sweater. When she arrived in Sal's bedroom, Travis was standing by her dressing table. He'd changed into jeans, too, and his favorite shirt, the one with the crown embroidered over his heart.

"Hi," she said, softly, feeling shy all of a sudden.

Travis pulled open a drawer and took out a small velvet box. "Come here, sweetheart. I've got something for you."

"Yes, boss." She moved closer. "What is it?"

Opening the box, he showed her the diamond ring nestled inside. "Great-Grandmother Rule's engagement ring. Another old family tradition. Every Rule bride wears this ring until the wedding. Then she gets one of her own, and this one goes back in the drawer.'' He slipped it on her finger. ''There's something else you need to know about the ring—''

''Here you are! I've been looking all over for you. Have you fired her yet?'' Stephanie walked into the room. She'd changed clothes, too. She was wearing a sheer black negligee, over a black satin gown.

''Stephanie,'' Travis groaned. He recovered quickly, taking Cindy by the hand. ''You can be the first to congratulate us. Cindy has agreed to be my wife.''

Stephanie's face turned a mottled red color. ''What did you say?''

''Cindy and I are engaged.''

''That's not possible. The contest—''

''—is over and Cindy won,'' Travis said.

Stephanie looked so shocked, so disbelieving, Cindy almost felt sorry for her. Until Stephanie turned her gaze from Travis to her. Her eyes glittered maliciously. ''Ellerbee. Congratulations,'' she managed to choke out.

''Thank you,'' said Travis. ''I appreciate your being a good sport about this.''

Cindy could only nod, chilled by the hatred she'd glimpsed in Stephanie's eyes before she'd gotten herself under control.

''Now, if you'll excuse us, we have plans to make.''

As soon as Stephanie withdrew, Travis let out a breath. ''Whew! I'm glad that's over. Don't ask her to be one of your bridesmaids, all right?''

''Bridesmaids? What kind of wedding are you planning?''

''A fast one. There's not much time left before my birthday. Now, where were we?''

"You'd just given me Great-Grandmother Rule's ring." Cindy held out her hand and admired the ring. "I love the old-fashioned setting."

"An occasion for a kiss, I'd say. Tell me again about my tempting mouth."

"I'd rather use it than talk about it." Cindy brushed her lips over his, then traced his mouth with the tip of her tongue.

Travis captured her tongue, sucking it deep into his mouth to play a sensuous game with his. When the kiss ended, he held her close. "Stephanie was right about one thing."

"Oh, yes? Her outfit, no doubt."

"That sheer black thing? I didn't notice. But get one like it for our wedding night, okay?"

She hit him on the shoulder.

"Ouch. But that's not what I meant. She was right about you needing to be fired. You're fired, Cindy."

"This makes the second time. I've only ever had two jobs, and I've been fired from both. Funny, this time I don't mind. I must be getting used to it."

"You can resign if you'd rather. But you can't work here anymore. You won't have time. We've got less than a week to plan a wedding. If I know Mom, she's going to whisk you off to San Antonio to shop. You'll need a wedding dress, and...stuff."

"Fae Rae is already looking for a replacement."

"And why is she doing that?"

"Because I asked her to. You didn't expect me to hang around and watch you marry someone else, did you? Is it all right if I invite her to the wedding?"

"Sure thing. You can invite anyone you like. Except Etienne."

"Etienne. I have to tell you about—"

The front door opened and closed, and several voices called out.

"Travis? Where are you?" asked Sal.

"Upstairs, Mom." Travis and Cindy hurriedly left the bedroom and descended the staircase.

"How was dinner?" Treat asked as he stood in the foyer with his mother and Brooke. "Hi, Cindy. You should have gone with us."

"Nope. You're wrong. Cindy's exactly where she's supposed to be. With me."

"Travis, dear, is there something we should know?"

"Cindy and I are going to get married."

Excitement surrounded her. Sal began laughing and crying at the same time. Treat slugged his brother on the shoulder, then wrapped him in a bear hug. Brooke hugged Cindy and wished her well. Travis kept her tucked next to his side, allowing the others to kiss and hug her, but never letting her go.

For all her years of wistful dreaming, Cindy had never imagined exactly how wonderful being loved would be.

Her happiness lasted until the next day.

Travis had put her to bed long after midnight. Wakening to a breakfast prepared by Travis and Treat, late the next morning, she'd been pampered and cosseted by everyone. Gus and the Ortegas had joined the family breakfast, and they'd added their good wishes, punctuated by more hugs and kisses.

Even Stephanie managed a peck on the cheek, before retiring to her room to pack.

After the meal was finished, including the clean-up in which Cindy had been forbidden to participate,

Treat offered to check on Stephanie. "I'll see if she's ready for a flight back to San Antonio."

"I'll go," said Travis. "I need to apologize for putting her through those tests."

Treat sat down at the kitchen table, where Cindy was staring out the window, holding a coffee cup filled with café au lait. She knew she had a silly grin on her face. She couldn't help it. She'd never been so happy.

"You're going to let him visit the black widow spider all alone?" teased Treat.

"What? Oh, yes."

"You trust him that much?"

Cindy nodded. "Of course. That's what love is all about. Trust." A tiny frown appeared on her forehead. "But I should apologize, too. I did pour champagne on her."

"You did what?"

"I poured champagne on Stephanie. And Travis. Her dress is probably ruined." Cindy stood up. "I must offer to replace it."

"Wait, I want to hear about the champagne bath."

"I'll tell you all about it. Later."

Cindy hurried up the stairs to Stephanie's room. The door was ajar, and she was about to push it open when she heard Stephanie's voice.

"I didn't make this up, Travis. I tell you your fiancée is a thief."

Cindy froze, her hand on the doorknob.

"Stephanie—"

"Listen to me. I called my friend Carolyn Hebert this morning. Caro lives in New Orleans, and she knows the people Cindy worked for. She told me the whole sordid story about why she left New Orleans.

Cindy seduced her employer's young susceptible brother, Etienne Breaux, and convinced him to give her an expensive engagement ring, a family heirloom. Just like the one you gave her, Travis.''

"I don't want to hear this, Stephanie," said Travis.

"You owe it to me to hear me out. Cindy must have realized that the family would never accept someone like her, a servant, a woman with no breeding, and so she switched the stone in the ring, substituting glass for the diamond. As luck would have it, Etienne came to his senses and asked her to return the ring. The theft was discovered, and she was fired. She would have gone to jail if she hadn't agreed to pay restitution. That's why she agreed to take on this job. She needed money.''

"Cindy wouldn't do that," insisted Travis.

"She did it once, and she's done it again. I saw the scratches with my own eyes. The stone in your great-grandmother's ring isn't a diamond, Travis. It's glass!''

Travis took Stephanie by the arm. "That does it. You're out of here." He pushed her, not too gently, toward the door.

"Travis, don't hate the messenger. Don't you see? She must have made the switch months ago, before she met you and decided the heir was better than the heirloom. The ring wasn't locked up, was it?''

"No, but you should be. Making accusations like that can get you in a lot of trouble, Stephanie. Keep moving.''

They reached the bottom of the stairs with Stephanie still pleading for Travis to come to his senses.

"What's going on?" asked Treat.

"Stephanie's leaving. Now.''

"Where's her luggage?"

"We'll pack it up and send it to her later. I want her gone."

"Treat, make him listen!" Stephanie grabbed Treat by his shirt, weeping hysterically.

"Listen to what?" asked Treat, a bewildered look on his face.

"Lies she's telling about Cindy."

"I'm not lying. It's the truth! She's a thief."

Sal and Brooke appeared in the foyer. "What's all the yelling about?" asked Sal.

Stephanie let go of Treat and threw herself at Sal. "Mrs. Rule! Sal! You'll believe me. That Ellerbee person has stolen the diamond from your family ring. And it's not the first time she's done something like that—"

Grabbing her by the shoulders, Sal held Stephanie away from her. "Calm down, Stephanie. What are you saying? That Cindy stole something?"

"A diamond! The stone in that engagement ring is glass!" wailed Stephanie, her voice shrill. "Get her in here. Look for yourself."

"That won't be necessary," said Sal, her voice cool, but calm. "Treat, why don't you take Stephanie back where she belongs?"

"My pleasure. Come on, Stephanie." Treat took her by the arm.

"Where's Cindy?" asked Travis suddenly. "I don't want her hearing that woman's accusations. Was she in the library with you?"

"No, dear," said Sal, "I haven't seen her since brunch. Brooke?"

"The last time I saw her was in the kitchen."

"Oh, my God!" Treat stopped in the doorway.

"She followed you upstairs, Travis. She wanted to tell Stephanie she was sorry she'd ruined her dress. She must have heard."

"And she ran," said Stephanie triumphantly. "The guilty always run, don't they?"

"Shut up, Stephanie. You don't know what you're talking about. Treat, go on. We'll find Cindy."

"I'll check her room," said Brooke.

"Maybe she's still upstairs." Sal headed for the stairway.

A quick but thorough search of the house proved unsuccessful. Cindy was nowhere to be found. "Maybe she's outside somewhere," said Travis, heading for the front door.

Treat was on the front steps. "The Bronco's gone."

"She drove away?" Travis shook his head. "I don't believe it. Where would she have gone? She's not that good a driver. Mom, what if she has an accident?"

"It's too soon to worry, Travis. I'll call Dolores. Maybe Cindy went there. Or to the bunkhouse."

The telephone calls proved as fruitless as the search. Dolores hadn't heard a car drive by, but she'd been vacuuming and the noise might have drowned out the sound of a passing car.

"I'm going to look for her," said Travis, jamming a Stetson on his head.

The telephone rang before he reached the door. Sal answered it. "Sheriff Jones! We were just about to call you. Have you seen Cindy Ellerbee?"

Cindy sat on the metal folding chair in the tiny office where the sheriff had put her. She never felt so alone and miserable. For a few hours, she'd had her dream, everything she'd ever wanted—the man she loved, his wonderful family—and she'd thrown it all away.

She stared at the ring on her finger. How had the diamond been switched? She hadn't done it. But no one would believe that. The ring hadn't been locked up. It had been right there in Sal's dresser drawer all those months she'd been alone at the ranch house.

Her heart broke when she thought about how Travis had refused to believe Stephanie. But he'd have to believe her once he saw the ring. He'd have no choice. There were tiny scratches on the faceted stone. She could see them, now that Stephanie had revealed their existence.

The sheriff had said she was only charged with making an illegal U-turn. He'd assured her she would be free to go as soon as he checked with the Rules to make sure she had permission to drive the Bronco. She didn't of course. She *was* a thief—she had taken the car without permission.

In her panic, she'd foolishly decided to cover up the crime she'd been falsely accused of. She'd planned to drive to the nearest jewelry store and have the glass stone replaced by a diamond. She had her savings account book with her, and she'd hoped the balance would pay for the substitution.

It wouldn't have worked. She'd figured that out before she'd been stopped by the police. She'd been on her way back to the ranch, to face Stephanie's accusations and to deny them. But that wouldn't have worked, either.

Once a thief, always a thief.

That's what Travis would have believed. She'd lost

her chance at happiness the minute Stephanie had discovered her past. Travis would wonder why she hadn't told him about the ring Etienne had given her, about the Frerets—

One of the deputies appeared at the office door. "You have visitors."

Her stomach clenched, and tiny beads of sweat appeared on her forehead. The nightmare was happening all over again. The confrontation, the accusations. Travis and his family would unite in condemning her. Only this time it would hurt a thousand times more, because this time she'd almost become one of them.

"Cindy, are you all right?" Travis pushed past the deputy and entered the office. She was in his arms before she had a chance to say a word.

"Sheriff Jones, really! Surely it wasn't necessary to lock Cindy up. She's not a criminal!" Sal scolded as she followed Travis into the room.

"She's not locked up, Miz Rule—the door was only closed," the deputy replied, wiping his brow with a bandanna.

"Buck up, Cindy gal, we're here to break you out of this joint," Brooke said, grinning at her as she squeezed into the small place.

"Anyone should be able to take one look at you and know you're not a thief!" said Travis, holding her so tight she could barely breathe.

Cindy was passed from one person to another, smothered in kisses and hugs. "You poor thing!" said Sal, patting her on the shoulder.

"Why did you do it Cindy?" asked Travis.

"I—I didn't."

"You ran away from me. Didn't you know I'd take

care of whatever was wrong? What *was* wrong? You haven't changed your mind, have you?''

"Oh, no. I love you."

"Let's go and do whatever paperwork needs to be done to straighten this out, shall we?'' asked Sal. "The sheriff said something about a traffic ticket." Sal and Brooke left the office, followed by the deputy.

"I love you, too, sweetheart," said Travis, once they were alone.

"I didn't steal from the Frerets."

"I know that. You couldn't have thought I'd believe Stephanie."

"To tell the truth, I didn't think. I panicked. I couldn't figure out how or when the stone was switched. So I decided I'd take the ring to a jeweler and have a diamond substituted for the glass stone."

Travis surprised her by laughing out loud. "That would have been the first time that setting contained a real diamond. Cindy, I should have told you—I meant to, but I never got around to it. Great-Grandmother Rule's ring has always been glass. That's why no one gets to wear it for long. It's too fragile."

Cindy stared at the ring. "Always glass?"

"Always. We weren't always wealthy, Cindy. Great-Grandfather Rule couldn't afford a diamond. But that ring symbolized the love all the Rule men feel for their women. So it became a tradition."

"There you go again, with that 'your woman' business."

"Get used to it, Cindy." He kissed her soundly. "You really must have panicked. If you'd been thinking, you would have realized no one would believe

Stephanie. I mean, why would you steal a diamond when you're about to marry—''

"The Richest Bachelor in Texas?"

"If I'm rich, it's only because you love me, Cindy Ellerbee. Cindyeller. My own Cinderella. I'm no Prince Charming, though, claiming my love with a glass slipper.''

Cindy threw herself into his arms.

"No, my prince claimed me with a glass ring."

# *Epilogue*

Fae Rae's round face glowed with pleasure. "You are a beautiful bride, Cindy. We knew you would be." Giving Cindy's veil one last pat, she turned to Sal. "Don't you agree, Mrs. Rule?"

"I certainly do. Travis is a very lucky man. All of us are. We're very lucky you sent Cindy to us, Fae Rae."

"I can't take all the credit. Benny had something to do with it, too."

"Benny?"

"My husband."

"Oh, I thought you were a widow."

"Yes, that's right." Fae Rae handed Cindy her bouquet of white roses. "When you think about it, Cindy, Etienne and the Frerets have something to do with this day, too. If Etienne hadn't stolen the diamond from his sister's ring, if she hadn't believed his lies—at least until he tried it again and got caught with his hand in her jewelry box—you'd still be in New Orleans."

"With a needlework shop in the Quarter." Cindy smiled. That dream had served its purpose, and she didn't regret losing it. Her dream of family had come true. "I never thought I'd be glad I was accused of theft, but you're right. Except for that, I wouldn't be here.''

"I like to think Travis would have found you, anyway,'' said Sal. ''It might have taken longer, though. This way, he found the woman he loves before his thirty-fifth birthday, and the Rule family tradition is intact.''

There was a knock on the door, and Mr. Rule entered. ''Ready?'' he asked, smiling fondly at Cindy.

Cindy nodded, the lump in her throat keeping her silent. She never could have dreamed such a perfect wedding day. Travis's father was going to give her away. Brooke was her maid of honor, and Treat the best man. Fae Rae and Sal, the Ortegas, Gus and the cowboys were the wedding guests.

Taking her soon-to-be father-in-law by the arm, Cindy let him lead her down the stairs to the library, where her Texas Prince waited.

\* \* \* \* \*

In **July 1998** comes

# THE MACKENZIE FAMILY

**by *New York Times* bestselling author**

# LINDA HOWARD

## The dynasty continues with:

**Mackenzie's Pleasure:** Rescuing a pampered ambassador's daughter from her terrorist kidnappers was a piece of cake for navy SEAL Zane Mackenzie. It was only afterward, when they were alone together, that the real danger began....

**Mackenzie's Magic:** Talented trainer Maris Mackenzie was wanted for horse theft, but with no memory, she had little chance of proving her innocence or eluding the real villains. Her only hope for salvation? The stranger in her bed.

*Available this July for the first time ever in a two-in-one trade-size edition. Fall in love with the Mackenzies for the first time—or all over again!*

Available at your favorite retail outlet.

*Silhouette* Books

# Take 4 bestselling love stories FREE

## Plus get a FREE surprise gift!

## Special Limited-time Offer

**Mail to Silhouette Reader Service™**

3010 Walden Avenue
P.O. Box 1867
Buffalo, N.Y. 14269-1867

**YES!** Please send me 4 free Silhouette Yours Truly™ novels and my free surprise gift. Then send me 4 brand-new novels every other month, which I will receive months before they appear in bookstores. Bill me at the low price of $2.90 each plus 25¢ delivery and applicable sales tax, if any.* That's the complete price and a savings of over 10% off the cover prices—quite a bargain! I understand that accepting the books and gift places me under no obligation ever to buy any books. I can always return a shipment and cancel at any time. Even if I never buy another book from Silhouette, the 4 free books and the surprise gift are mine to keep forever.

201 SEN CF2X

| Name | (PLEASE PRINT) | |
| --- | --- | --- |
| Address | Apt. No. | |
| City | State | Zip |

This offer is limited to one order per household and not valid to present Silhouette Yours Truly™ subscribers. *Terms and prices are subject to change without notice. Sales tax applicable in N.Y.

USYRT-296

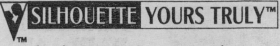